Janet McNaughton

HarperTrophyCanada™
An imprint of HarperCollins*Publishers*Ltd

Published by Harper*Trophy*Canada™, an imprint of
HarperCollins Publishers Ltd.

Originally published in Canada in a hardcover edition by
HarperCollins Publishers Ltd: 2011
This Harper*Trophy*Canada™ trade paperback edition: 2012

Harper*Trophy*Canada™ is a registered trademark of HarperCollins Publishers.

HarperCollins books may be purchased for educational, business, or sales
promotional use through our Special Markets Department.

HarperCollins Publishers Ltd
2 Bloor Street East, 20th Floor
Toronto, Ontario, Canada
M4W 1A8

www.harpercollins.ca

Library and Archives Canada Cataloguing in Publication
information is available upon request

ISBN 978-1-44340-678-9

Printed and bound in the United States

RRD 9 8 7 6 5 4 3

For Nathaniel Oppel

CHAPTER ONE

DRAGON DREAMS

Safe in his red-brick lair in the heart of the city, the dragon dreams, nose to toes, his tail draped over his neck like a scarf. A wisp of snow-chilled air seeps under the wooden door. His crest rises to register pleasure, then falls again, like a sigh. He hears sleigh bells and the steady hiss of metal runners on hard-packed snow, laughter ringing out over spruce-clad hills. He sees Daniel, bent over his notebook in the mellow lamplight of a ship's cabin, hears canvas sails snap like dragons' wings in the wind. His dreams fall backward in time, swiftly, over centuries until, finally, the sharp scent of a charcoal fire tickles his nose and he hears the musical *tink* of a tiny hammer in the glow of a bronze-smith's forge. Then, he is a hatchling, sitting in the sun on a beach with his clutch mates and cousins, watching

1

the big dragons fly; his beautiful mother, his wise father, his mother's funny sister and her mate, only four of them, but they know everything. Looking down, he can see the blood veins running through his sharp grey claws, white sand clinging to them, the memory crisp in every detail, though it is more than a thousand years old.

Even as a hatchling, even in a happy moment on the beach, he already knew to keep watch for the Vikings' wooden boats. Much later, he would learn they were called *Drakkar*, dragon ships. That made him shake his head. The Vikings hated the dragons, tried to kill his father, caused the chain of events that left him the last of his kind. The Vikings ruined anything they touched.

Fast asleep in his chilly lair, the dragon rolls away from these troubling memories. Teetering on the brink of dreams, he wonders where Daniel is. He'd said he'd be back in a few weeks. Surely the time has passed. The thought forms and vanishes as the dragon slips once more into his enchanted sleep.

In fact, Daniel has been gone for one hundred and twelve years.

BIRD NERD

A hard wind blew off the North Atlantic, shrinking Gwyn into the warmth of his down jacket. The ocean was out of sight, just beyond the hills on the other side of the lake. He could picture it, an icy, heaving expanse of black water stretching all the way from Newfoundland to Europe. Somewhere out there a storm was brewing. He could feel it in his bones.

Gwyn glanced at the mouth of the Virginia River beside him again, looking for the birds he'd come to see, two male wood ducks. The Latin name for wood duck, *Aix sponsa*, meant "waterbird in bridal clothes." Linnaeus, the Swedish scientist who gave them that name in the 1700s, had been making a joke, and Gwyn always got it when he saw them. Though they wintered with the mallards and black ducks like part of the gang, they looked as if they should be in some kind of bird fashion show. Bird books would tell you that Nova Scotia was the northernmost edge of their habitat; even so, it wasn't unusual for them to show up on Quidi Vidi in the winter. They were nowhere today, though. Gwyn was disappointed but not alarmed. Ducks could disappear for days at a time, up the Virginia River running into the lake beside him, or the Rennie's River closer to home, or even downstream into Quidi Vidi Harbour.

Gwyn checked his watch. Only four-thirty and night was already creeping in from the sea. At least January was almost over. Time to go home. He pulled his binoculars from the warmth of his jacket for a quick look at the gulls in the middle of the lake before he went. This calm lake, so close to the open sea, was a haven for odd birds that had been storm-tossed to this side of the Atlantic or were just plain lost. Birders actually flew to St. John's in winter just to see the Bonaparte's gulls and Icelandic gulls that showed up here.

"Hey, Rae!"

Gwyn's body tensed to the threatening tone even before he recognized the voice. Oh no, Tyler Cull. This was not good. Gwyn stuffed the binoculars (expensive, breakable) into his jacket before turning, and was almost knocked off his feet by a big, black dog. Fat and smelly, it lumbered by on skinny legs, wheezing with effort. Gwyn was no fan of dogs, and this one seemed more repulsive than most. It flopped into the Virginia River, scattering ducks in all directions. Then it stood ankle-deep in the middle of the river, looking stupidly pleased with itself.

"Call your dog off," Gwyn shouted. "You're not supposed to let it run around off leash on this trail." In that moment of fury, he forgot who he was talking to. Though they were both twelve, Tyler Cull was a head taller. And mean.

Tyler stopped in amazement, raised one eyebrow, then smiled as if he'd just been handed a present. "Run around off leash? Who do you think you are, my nan?" He took a step forward.

Gwyn was cornered. He'd have to run across the river to escape, scaring the ducks that were just beginning to settle again. He'd be no better than the dog if he did that.

He chose to stay.

The dog came back up the bank, spraying cold water everywhere.

"Good boy, Cuddles," Tyler said absently.

Cuddles. Gwyn had to bite his lip to keep from smiling.

Tyler took his time, clearly enjoying himself as he picked a particularly vicious-looking chunk of ice before advancing on Gwyn.

That's cheating, Gwyn thought. Then he almost laughed. Why would anyone like Tyler Cull play fair?

The inward chuckle must have made it as far as his face. Tyler's eyes narrowed to slits. "I'm going to turn that face into hamburger," he growled.

Past his attacker's shoulder, Gwyn saw a middle-aged woman walking a shitzu. The dog looked like a dust mop on a leash. He grabbed the chance.

"Aunt Judy," Gwyn cried, brushing past Tyler. He ran to the woman's side and stopped in mock confusion. "Oh," he said. "You aren't my aunt."

The woman gave him a puzzled smile.

"Is that a shitzu?" Gwyn asked, as if it really mattered to him. He ransacked his mind for something, anything to get the woman talking so he could walk away from Tyler Cull with her. He put his hand out to pat the little dog, but it disappeared behind its owner with a whimper. Smart dog, thought Gwyn, and the fact he needed came to him, something he'd read in one of his father's genetics journals a few weeks before.

"Did you know," he said, "that shitzus are more closely related to wolves than larger dogs like German shepherds?" and he began to walk.

"Really?" The woman fell into step beside him. Gwyn resisted the urge to glance back at Tyler Cull, while he strained to remember more about what he'd read.

A few minutes later, when Gwyn left the woman at King's Bridge Road, he had to make a quick decision.

Across the road, the trail followed the Rennie's River in the direction of home. Gwyn would be alone if Tyler caught him there, but it was faster. There was a break in the traffic, so Gwyn jogged across the street, letting the tree-lined trail swallow him.

It was always quiet here. The river ran black in winter between snowy banks. The houses on either side were distanced by long backyards so it was hard to remember he was near the heart of the city. When he was younger, this wooded trail had overflowed with magic, dragons and unicorns waiting at every bend in the river. One summer, there had been an evil Viking wizard who could take the shape of a crow. Gwyn had almost forgotten how he and his sister, Maddie, had terrified themselves with that one, running and screaming whenever a crow landed near them. Where had that come from? It must have been something they'd read or seen on TV. Gwyn smiled, then his smile slipped away like the fading light. Once, he'd thought those days of make-believe would last forever. Now he knew better.

Most days, Gwyn would have looked for birds in the trees overhead or on the river. Now he kept his eyes on his feet to help him navigate the icy path while a flood tide of darkness rose around him. I'm scurrying home like a small, hunted creature, he thought, a mouse or maybe a rat. I wish I could be brave enough to face guys like Tyler instead of always running.

Near his own neighbourhood, Gwyn dashed onto the street, then switched to the maze of back lanes. He smiled. Only kids raised in Georgetown knew the lanes existed. If Tyler Cull was still looking for him, he wouldn't find a trace. He passed the backyards of oddly mixed wooden houses, some of them lovingly tended by their owners, others fallen into disrepair. Gwyn's own street was the oddest in the neighbourhood. Two blocks were pure Georgetown, with plain wooden row houses hugging the sidewalks. The third (and final) block held four big Victorian mansions with lawns and trees, each unique, facing property owned by the Catholic Church. That last block, Gwyn's block, looked as if it belonged to a different part of the city.

By the time Gwyn reached his house night had fallen, solid and black. He slipped, like a thief, down the driveway and into the safety of his own kitchen. Only then did he let out the breath he'd been holding since he'd left the lake. At least it was Friday. He wouldn't have to worry about Tyler for two whole days.

The house was dark, and Gwyn wondered why Maddie wasn't home, then he remembered. Soccer. In her first year of high school, Maddie had already made the school team for indoor soccer. This surprised no one. Maddie was a natural athlete. She was a natural at everything. Good at sports, good at making friends, good at school—

everything Gwyn was not. It had probably always been that way, but Gwyn had never noticed until this year. Maybe because, along with everything else, Maddie was good at being a sister.

She came in a few minutes later, her long, dark hair still pulled back for soccer, glowing from the game. Maddie loved sports so much it didn't matter to her if her teams won, though they usually did.

"How was the game?" Gwyn asked.

"Oh, we won. Twelve to three." Then she frowned. "Megan Morrissey, the captain, is moving. Her mother's been transferred to Alberta. This was her last game. It's really too bad." She sounded upset.

"Was she a friend of yours?" Gwyn asked.

Maddie seemed to be thinking about something else. "What? Oh, no. She's in grade twelve. I barely knew her." She sighed. "She was fair though, and that counts."

It sounded as if something was going on, but Gwyn let it go. Maddie was harder to understand now that she was a teenager. If she wanted him to know, she'd tell him.

At least he could still talk to Maddie about his problems, tell her things he'd keep from their parents—like what had happened today.

"Tyler Cull almost got me by Quidi Vidi after school."

"I remember him. He's almost twice your size. What were you fighting about?"

"His stupid dog scared all the ducks down at the lake." It seemed silly now. Would Maddie laugh?

"What an idiot! Dogs aren't supposed to be off leash on that trail."

Gwyn smiled. "That's right. It made me so mad, I yelled at him."

"Who, Tyler or the dog?"

This made Gwyn laugh. "Tyler."

"You want a snack?" Maddie asked. She was not the sort of sister to gush or fuss, and Gwyn knew this was her way of being kind.

"Peanut butter and jelly?" he replied, because she was also not the sort of sister who could do much in the kitchen.

"Oh, we're supposed to take pizza dough out of the fridge," Maddie said, reading the note on the door. "Good thing I noticed."

A few minutes later she set a plate in front of him. "You've got to be more careful, Gwyn. What if he goes after you at school? I'm not there to defend you any more."

"I shouldn't need you to defend me." Gwyn sighed. "I wish I had a big pet, bigger than Tyler's old dog. Something fierce, like the Rae dragon. Just imagine. If I had a dragon, I'd never have to worry about getting beat up. It would breathe fire all over them and they'd be toast."

Maddie smiled. "I remember the first time I heard about the dragon," she said. "It was Christmas Eve, and you were really little but not a baby so I must have been about four. It seemed so late, and you were already asleep on the couch by the fire. I was too wound up to sleep. How could Santa get down the chimney if we had a fire? What if he got burned? Dad finally got out that ancient manuscript, to distract me I guess, and told me how our family came to look after the dragon. He said the Vikings wanted to slay the fierce dragons and our ancestors were only able to save one—"

"And they cared for the dragon," Gwyn added, letting himself be swept up by the magic of the story.

"—because that was what they did," Maddie finished.

"That's exactly the kind of pet I need. Whatever happened to that dragon?"

Maddie sighed. "I don't know. I remember asking Dad how the dragon got to Newfoundland. He just laughed."

"How *did* the dragon get to Newfoundland?" Gwyn asked, waiting to see if Maddie would play along. Did she remember the magic? Now that she was fourteen, that part of their friendship was slipping away, leaving Gwyn alone in an empty place.

"Well, the Rae dragon must have come from Scotland in 1887 with our great-great-uncle, the Reverend Daniel Rae, because our great-grandfather was only a baby when he came over ten years later. It's all on that family tree Gran made." The one Maddie still had on her bedroom wall. So she was not too old to play this game.

Gwyn smiled. "How would a clergyman look after a dragon?" he asked.

Maddie sat down beside him with her own snack. "He didn't have a choice, did he? Our family always cared for the dragon. And we know he was responsible. When his younger brother died, he arranged to bring the widow and her baby son to Newfoundland so they wouldn't live as paupers in Scotland. He was so responsible, he went to Boston to meet them. And, on his way, the ship sank and he died."

"But Agatha Rae and her baby came here anyway," Gwyn prompted. He liked to hear the story, even if it was sad.

"Yes, they did. Their passage to Newfoundland was already arranged and everything was ready for them here. A wealthy builder had provided a house and the congregation cared for them just as if Daniel hadn't died. They even bought her a piano so she could give music lessons. When she finally remarried, her son, Hamish, didn't change his last name, out of respect for his brave Uncle Daniel. Which is why we are named Rae, but the other relatives on our father's side are Bairds."

"And we're the only ones with a dragon," Gwyn concluded.

They munched in comfortable silence for a few minutes while Gwyn thought.

"You know," he said at last, "Daniel was planning to come back from Boston. I bet he left the dragon somewhere safe. I bet we could find it if we tried."

Now Maddie did laugh. "I don't know about that, Gwyn." Then she added, "Do you have any homework?"

She was her willing herself to sound casual. She even pretended to look out the window, though night pressed against the glass, hiding everything. Gwyn said nothing as he struggled with his temper. Maddie was just about the only friend he had right now. He'd be lost if they fought. Still, he knew what she was up to. He'd accidentally overheard the night before when Maddie and their mother were filling the dishwasher. Gwyn had been about to bring a load of dirty plates into the kitchen when the sound of his own name had stopped him out of sight by the doorway.

" . . . grade seven could be Gwyn's crash and burn year if this keeps up," his mother was saying. "His homeroom teacher was worried enough to call me at work. 'Can't do worse than zero,' he said. Gwyn's not even passing in assignments. I feel like I hardly know him these days." The catch in his mother's voice made Gwyn's ear burn. He was backing away quietly when he heard one more thing. "Would you try to help him, Maddie? He still looks up to you."

Gwyn knew that most sisters, at fourteen, would have made excuses or at least complained. But Maddie didn't hesitate. "I'll see what I can do, Mom."

Gwyn turned away quickly, almost spilling the flatware as he left the stack of dirty plates on the table. A swirl of emotions chased him up to his attic bedroom. It was true—he wasn't doing his schoolwork. If he was so grown up, like everyone kept telling him, shouldn't it be his own business?

Suddenly, his life seemed pointless. Last spring, Gwyn had decided he was too old to spend the summer geeking out with Dad. Maddie had bailed out of the family summer science project a few years before so now it was his turn. The way his father had accepted this decision, struggling to conceal his disappointment, had left Gwyn with a hole in the pit of his stomach, but by then it was too late to take it back. And lying around all summer had turned out to be no fun at all.

Junior high was supposed to be this big step forward. Nothing they taught, *nothing*, had anything to do with becoming a bird biologist. Meanwhile Gwyn's friends, some he'd known since kindergarten, had disappeared into computer games, one by one. What made them want to sit in darkened rooms for hours, killing and dying on the computer screen over and over? The world outside was so amazing, so *real*. Couldn't they see that? They'd all gone weird, too, trying to be just like everyone else, shunning anyone who seemed different. It was like they'd turned into clones.

Junior high was not a party. It was more like a prison with lots of nasty, strangely similar inmates. And Gwyn had somehow gone from being the bright kid who did better than anyone else to the weird kid at the bottom of the class. There were words for what he was now and they all began with L—loser, loner, lonely, lost. He didn't like it. And he was trapped.

"Gwyn? I said, do you have any homework?" Maddie's voice jerked him back to the present.

He lifted his backpack from the floor. It suddenly seemed incredibly heavy. If anyone but Maddie had been asking . . . this *was* Maddie, though. He rummaged inside the pack until he found a crumpled paper and pushed it across the table, a little harder than he'd intended. "Mr. Banfield said I could bring my history grade up to a pass if I do a good job on this."

Maddie smoothed the creases, squinting at the print. "Oh," she said, "the Heritage Fair. I remember that from grade seven. It could be . . . great."

Gwyn had to stop himself from wincing. She was forcing herself to sound excited.

"No, really," Maddie continued, as if she'd read his mind. "You could do something fun. I'd help."

"Something fun? What would that be?" He couldn't resist pushing a little before he gave in.

"I don't know," Maddie began. Then her face lit up. "You could do it on Daniel Rae. Or Agatha and Hamish. It's a great story, and Gran had all those old family papers. She was always showing me stuff after Grandpa died."

Gwyn was so surprised, he sat back in his chair. "That would be interesting," he heard himself say. Even though he was playing right into his mother's hands, the look on Maddie's face—pure delight, with no trace of triumph— made it okay. Besides, maybe he could find out more about the Rae dragon.

CHAPTER THREE

Λ Promise

"Is there dessert?" Maddie asked a few hours later. They sat around the big old dining-room table, the wreckage of homemade pizza and salad on their plates.

Her mother smiled. "We may have some of your father's blueberry coffee cake in the freezer. Let's check." Maddie and her mother collected the plates and disappeared into the kitchen.

Gwyn looked out the dining room window, where a fierce wind whipped the trees against low clouds. His father followed his gaze. "There's a blizzard warning," Tom said. "We're supposed to get thirty centimetres tonight."

So he'd been right when he'd felt the storm coming. Gwyn sighed. It was a shame to waste a good blizzard on a Friday night. It should have meant a day off school.

17

School reminded him of the Heritage Fair. He'd forgotten about it while everyone chatted over supper.

"Where did Daniel Rae's papers go when Gran died?" he asked his father.

Tom eased back from the table before replying. A tall, bearded man, thin and athletic, he looked more like a field biologist than a geneticist who spent his life in the lab. "The family papers? Why do you want to know?" In some families, it would have been rude to answer a question with a question, but this didn't surprise Gwyn. His father was a true scientist, curious about everything, deliberate, patient and thorough. Gwyn still thought he was perfect.

"I'm going to do the Heritage Fair. Maybe Daniel Rae would make a good topic."

"Good idea. Come to the university some day after school and look in the newspapers. There's bound to be an obituary, and you can photocopy the articles about the shipwreck. There's loads of stuff in our family papers, too. Your great-great-grandmother Agatha saved all of Daniel's papers. She must have thought the world of her brother-in-law, even though they never met."

Gwyn wondered if she'd felt guilty about Daniel's death. If he hadn't gone to meet her, he wouldn't have died.

"Daniel was an amateur photographer, too," Gwyn's father continued. "There's a collection of photographs, and big stacks of his sermons and notebooks." Tom Rae sighed. "I guess the sudden death of such a talented person is always sad. He could have done so much more if he'd lived longer."

"How old was he?" Gwyn had always thought of his great-great-uncle as ancient.

"In his late thirties. Young to die, even for the nineteenth century."

"Is there enough for a Heritage Fair project?"

"More than enough."

"Great. Where are the family papers now?"

Again, his father seemed to deflect the question. "We had some long talks about this when your grandmother was making up her will. She felt the papers were too valuable to stay the way they were. She was afraid they might be scattered or neglected over the years. I was opposed to the idea at first, but eventually she won me over. The collection needed to be professionally conserved and organized and made available to researchers. I hated to let it go out of the family and I drew the line at the dragon manuscript. It must be hundreds of years old, and it had to stay with us. That and a box of mementoes are all we have now. They weren't suitable for the archives, just junk, really. The box is in my office. I'll bring it home for you next week. Everything else is in good hands."

"Where?" Gwyn was getting tired of repeating the question.

"Where is what?" His mother came back into the dining room with a pot of tea. Maddie followed with the cake and plates.

"The family papers, Annie. Gwyn's thinking of doing a Heritage Fair project on Daniel Rae."

For a split second, Gwyn's mother looked delighted. "Oh that's —" She caught Gwyn's expression mid-sentence and her voice fell flat. " —so nice."

Gwyn swallowed his annoyance and turned back to his father. "Where is everything?" he asked again.

Tom poured himself a cup of tea, giving his wife and Maddie a chance to settle before replying, then he gave Gwyn an odd look. "Where are the family papers, indeed. That's the question."

Maddie laughed. "You do know, don't you, Dad?"

"Of course he knows," her mother said. "They're in the Provincial Archives."

"Oh no. The Rooms." Maddie turned to Gwyn. "You're not going to give up on this just because the family papers are in The Rooms." It wasn't a question, it was a command.

The Heritage Fair project came crashing down around Gwyn's ears. "I promised I'd never go there."

"Yes, Gwyn, but who did you promise? Only yourself," his mother said gently. "And that must have been two years ago."

Three, Gwyn thought, though he said nothing. It was three years.

"Even if you manage to spent the rest of your life avoiding the art gallery, I don't see how you can do without the museum, and now you need the archives. The Heritage Fair is still a great idea," Maddie said. "Just think about it." She turned to their mother, changing the subject. "Do we have a movie?"

"Nothing you'll want to watch, Maddie. I didn't know about the blizzard warning when I picked it up," Annette replied. "I thought you'd be out with your friends."

Maddie bent her head so her hair curtained her face. "I didn't have plans. So what's the movie?"

"*The Wild Parrots of Telegraph Hill.*"

"Wow," Gwyn said. "That's great."

"Sounds fine to me." Maddie seemed to mean it, and Gwyn wondered why. She liked mushy romantic comedies. Documentaries about birds were at the bottom of her must-see list. "I'll make popcorn if you clear the rest of the dishes, Gwyn," she added.

"More food? We just ate," Tom protested.

His wife patted him on the shoulder. "She's a growing girl, dear. Do you need help with the popcorn maker, Maddie?"

"I can handle it," Maddie replied.

Gwyn cleared the table and began to fill the dishwasher while Maddie wrestled the old hot-air corn popper down from the top cupboard. "I wish I had a fencing mask," she muttered. She got a large colander, then measured the popcorn.

Gwyn smiled to himself. They owned a hot-air corn popper because their mother insisted. She was that sort of person. For example, she was Annette Prothero, not Annette Rae, too proud of her Welsh heritage to change her name when she married. A professional nutritionist with the hospital corporation, she had firm ideas about what should and should not be eaten and, in this house, her word was law. She'd banned microwave popcorn because of the trans fats and salt. Gwyn could not remember life without the noisy, unpredictable hot-air corn popper. He could always count on it to send a few kernels ricocheting across the kitchen mid-pop. Making popcorn was a bit like setting off fireworks indoors. It scared Gwyn, but he loved it anyway.

Once the corn popper was plugged in, they couldn't talk. Maddie stood by the counter like a firefighter waiting for the blaze. When popcorn started pouring into the colander, she gingerly shifted the hot kernels to keep them from overflowing. Gwyn sat at the kitchen table, waiting. Maddie's shoulders were just beginning to relax when a last kernel spilled out, popping as it hit the side of the colander. It flew to the wall beside the stove, dinging the wall clock square in the face, then bounced back. With her athlete's reflexes, Maddie ducked, and the stray kernel sailed over her head like a small, crazed cloud, impaling itself on the spout of the olive oil decanter on the counter.

"That," Gwyn said, "was awesome." It was easily the corn popper's best performance ever.

Maddie almost looked annoyed, then recovered. "Microwave popcorn is so boring."

Gwyn couldn't stop smiling as he divided the popcorn into bowls.

Gwyn's father had made a fire in the fireplace. It roared and crackled as sudden downdrafts hinted at the storm outside. The furniture was a bit shabby now, but nothing could hide the elegance of this room, with its high ceiling covered in elaborate plaster moulding. Maddie turned out the lights and flopped into her favourite chair, near her parents, who were already nestled together on the couch. Gwyn sprawled sideways on his chair, a big wingback, with a bowl of popcorn on his stomach. As the movie began, he wished it could always be Friday night with a blizzard to keep his family safe at home.

Gwyn forgot about the Heritage Fair until bedtime. Then, as he climbed into bed, he shrugged it off. The Rooms was only two blocks from his house, but he'd managed to avoid going inside since it opened last summer, even though he'd had to give up the provincial museum when it relocated there. The Heritage Fair was months away. He had plenty of time to sort out his feelings, time to decide if he wanted to look at those family papers badly enough to break the promise he'd made to himself. That night, though, he dreamed there was a huge iron key lying across the dining-room table. Even the floor creaked and groaned under the weight of it. "Take this key to The Rooms," a voice ordered. "Something's there for you. It's been waiting for centuries. Take this key and find it."

o o o

That was a weird one, Gwyn thought when he opened his eyes in the morning. The room was filled with storm light, his window curtained by swirls and eddies of falling snow, and he snuggled into the warm bed as he tried to puzzle out the dream. Nothing had been waiting in The Rooms for centuries, the place was brand new. His dream must have had something to do with Fort Townsend, the old fort that had once stood on the site of The Rooms — the reason he'd promised himself he'd never go there.

The aroma of fresh pancakes wafted up from the kitchen to tickle his nose, calling him out of his tangle of blankets and dreams.

He found his mother in the kitchen still in her house-coat and pyjamas, reading a novel. "Pancake batter in the fridge," she said without looking up. "Help yourself."

Gwyn glanced at the half-finished shopping list on the fridge. Normally, his parents would have been at the supermarket by now. "Everything closed?" he asked.

Annette put her book down. "Snowed in, good and proper. Twenty centimetres, I'd guess, and falling. Nobody's going anywhere until this is ploughed out. And Sunny won't be driving in from Portugal Cove for dinner."

Gwyn buried his nose in the fridge so his mother couldn't read his relief. Sunny Goodman and Annette Prothero had been best friends since first year university, but no one could figure out why. Sunny had an amazing ability to say the wrong thing, and her emotional upheavals could demand his mother's full attention for days at a time. Once, just once, when they were alone in the car together, Tom had said, "This is the thing about Sunny — she takes up more space than she fills." Somehow that made sense to Gwyn, even though he didn't exactly understand it.

As Gwyn poured some pancake batter, his mother continued. "It's a shame. I haven't seen Sunny in ages, and she was anxious to tell us about that new Viking dig she oversaw at L'Anse aux Meadows last summer. She said they made some spectacular finds."

That piqued Gwyn's curiosity. Sunny's profession, archaeology, was easily her best feature. "What, cloak pins and stuff?" His family visited the Viking site at L'Anse aux Meadows, at the northern tip of the island, every few summers, even though the trip took days. It was the only place in North America where a Viking settlement had ever been found, and people came from all over the world to see it.

"More than cloak pins. Sunny said they found things they'd never seen before. We'll just have to wait to find out."

Gwyn didn't want to wait. "Maybe she could come for supper tomorrow."

Annette laughed. "You're not usually anxious to see Sunny. I'll call her later and ask." She shook her head. "You guys and your fascination with Vikings. If I didn't know the Raes came from Scotland, I'd think you had Norse ancestors."

"Gran said we might have, farther back than she could trace, didn't she? She said lots of Vikings came into Scotland at different times."

"That's a funny thing to remember."

"Maddie and I use to talk about it." Gwyn had never told his mother about the dread that was mixed with his fascination. For him, Vikings were as scary as vampires. Even here, in this bright, cozy kitchen, he shuddered.

While he flipped his pancakes, Gwyn wondered what to do. Being snowed in for an evening was fine, but a whole day was too boring. He remembered the Heritage Fair and suddenly knew where he had to go to sort himself out.

"I think I'll snowshoe around the lake," he said as he sat down to eat.

"Good idea. There won't be any traffic to worry about. Just watch for the ploughs if they hit the roads before you get back."

Gwyn sighed. His mother just couldn't stop acting like a mother.

◦ ◦ ◦

Half an hour later, Gwyn stepped outside in full winter hiking gear. He hadn't worn his weatherproof snow pants since Maddie had called them "the geek's idea of high fashion." They were perfect now, though, keeping the snow out of his boots as he struggled over a drift to the street. The hard edges of the city were gone, softened and sculpted by freshly fallen snow. Gwyn's snowshoes were the high-tech, lightweight kind with cleats on the bottom that made them clumsy on cleared streets, so he'd usually carry them in a backpack to the lake and put them on there. Today, though, because there was nothing *but* snow, he stumbled back to the front steps, sat on a cushion of snow and strapped them on.

Though the wind raged high above, here at street level everything was hushed and muffled. It was easy to imagine the houses away. Trekking up the middle of the street, Gwyn pretended he was John Rae, the intrepid Arctic explorer, the only human being for miles. Wrapped in these dreams of adventure, he made it all the way to the lake before he remembered why he'd come here.

He looked at the bridge that crossed the Rennie's River where it flowed into the lake. He'd found out about The Rooms on that very spot, three years before, while helping with the Christmas Bird Count for the first time. He'd been nine, and he'd begged his parents to let him be part of the Count for weeks. It had been going on all over North America for more than a century without him and he couldn't stand to let one more year go by.

The day came back in vivid detail. Gwyn had stood with his elbows on the railing to steady his field glasses while an icy wind knifed in off the ocean, making his whole face ache. He'd never been allowed out alone with adults who were strangers before and he'd been afraid to talk to them at first, in case he said something dumb. The two birders were graduate students in archaeology, a young couple from Ontario and Quebec, Greg and Angelique. Gwyn had been warned he might have to bring one of his parents along if no one wanted to be paired with a kid. These students could have refused to take him out with them, but they'd treated him like an equal from the start, and soon they were talking like old friends.

They knew Sunny, of course, and after a few hours they started to talk about archaeology. That was when The Rooms came up.

"They're putting that new museum, art gallery and archive complex right over the ruins of Fort Townsend," Greg told Gwyn. Though they were both looking at the lake with binoculars, the outrage in Greg's voice made his feelings clear. "You wouldn't believe how big that fort was. They should preserve at least some of it, make it part of the attraction."

That sounded reasonable to Gwyn. "Why don't they?"

"Ask *them*," Greg said, his voice bitter.

"Really, Gwyn, you should see the historic plans," Angelique added. "It was just like the Halifax Citadel. Such a loss. These people, they throw their heritage away." She said "t'row." Her accent charmed Gwyn. "Even though those British built that fort mainly to keep my ancestors out of Newfoundland, it deserves better," she concluded.

They took Gwyn birding a few more times, and later that winter, they showed him the plans of the old fort, included in a study commissioned by the government that had been smuggled out of the Confederation Building by angry archaeologists. Greg and Angelique were right. The fort had been beautiful, star-shaped and huge. The site should have been excavated by archaeologists and preserved for everyone to see. Instead, that following summer, the ruins had been bulldozed to make way for The Rooms.

Greg and Angelique had graduated and moved on. Now, it seemed everyone simply accepted the destruction of the old fort. Everyone except Gwyn. He had never gone into The Rooms, and never expected to.

His memories took him a quarter of the way around the lake without seeing anything. Finally, Gwyn looked up. The lake was veiled in curtains of falling snow, yesterday's grey ice now a vast coverlet. It was just cold enough to keep the snow fluffy. Gwyn was warm and dry inside his winter gear. He was now opposite where he'd met Tyler Cull the day before. This part of the trail was nearer to the ocean but sheltered by hills from the worst of the winds so it was covered with trees and thickets. Songbirds nested here in summer, and those that wintered found refuge from the weather. Gwyn was walking a metre above where his feet would have been in summer. I wish someone would just tell me what to do, he thought as he walked. No, I don't, he told himself immediately. I'm too old for that. I just wish I knew.

He slowed his pace to look for birds in the branches and there they were—a flock that looked like sparrows who'd gotten into red ink. Jittery, twittery birds who could not keep still or silent for a second. They dashed from a low thicket to a snowbank and disappeared. Gwyn smiled. Redpolls. They were the only birds he knew who made tunnels in the snow to keep warm in winter, and he'd only seen them do that once before. Redpolls didn't nest here, and they usually stayed in the same place all year round, but a sudden food shortage could send them flocking to a completely different location. They'd move all the way from Labrador to Newfoundland if that happened.

The redpolls filled Gwyn with unexpected happiness—even birds could change when they had to. Staying out of The Rooms had seemed right until yesterday. Now, he really wanted to see those family papers. His snowshoes carried him toward home with a spring in his step and the hope that the future might hold good things. He remembered what his mother had said the night before. He'd only promised *himself* he wouldn't go into The Rooms. Maybe it was okay to break a promise to yourself if you had a good reason.

Chapter Four

The Rooms

Gwyn's decision felt less comfortable the next day as he slogged to The Rooms with Maddie. The building was practically around the corner from their house, but overnight the snowploughs had turned snow-white fields into salt-slushed roads and high, lumpy snowbanks. The sun was so bright it hurt.

When they reached the massive building, Gwyn stopped walking. "Maybe this isn't such a good idea—" he began.

Maddie cut him off. "You can't change your mind now."

She couldn't boss him around like that. Gwyn flung his arm at the huge pile of glass and steel and stone. "Look at it," he cried. "You can see it from all over the city. It's hideous. Tourists have stopped me in the Battery to ask,

'What's that ugly building?' And they ruined an archaeological site to build it. An important one."

Maddie sighed. "Most people have forgotten about Fort Townsend, Gwyn. Things would be easier if you could be like everyone else."

Gwyn exploded. "What kind of world would it be if everyone was the same?" He went on, answering his own question. "A world of clones. A world of drones. No imagination. No science. No change. I can't believe you said that."

A family on the steps leading to The Rooms turned to stare at him. Gwyn didn't care.

Maddie stared too, saying nothing, and it seemed Gwyn had hit harder than he'd intended.

"You're right," she finally said. "Nobody should try to make you into something you're not." She turned away from The Rooms. "Let's go home." This wasn't a ploy. She sounded completely defeated.

"Wait!" Gwyn's confusion rooted him to the spot. This wasn't like Maddie at all. "Wait," he said more gently. All the reasons he wanted to do this project came back to him. "I shouldn't have yelled at you. It's just hard to give in, you know?" He took a deep breath. "It's okay, I'll do it." He started up the steps before he could change his mind again.

Maddie came into the lobby just as Gwyn was being directed upstairs to the archives. She paid at the desk before she caught up with him, even though the woman who took her money told her they didn't need to pay to use the archives.

Gwyn was relieved he wouldn't have to explain himself to strange adults alone, and more relieved to know they weren't fighting. He looked around at the massive sheets of glass that went right up to the roof to create a huge atrium, bisected by staircases and landings. The place was mostly empty today and it had the hushed air of a cathedral. "It's nicer on the inside," he said as they climbed the stairs.

Maddie smiled. "That's what everyone says."

The archives was divided by banks of desks, cabinets and microfilm readers. It seemed empty. "I don't think anyone's here," Gwyn said.

"Is someone there?" A woman's head popped up from behind a bank of cabinets. "Goodness," she said, "I wasn't expecting anyone today after all that snow. All the other staff stayed home." She came over to them, a tall, thin woman with grey hair. "I'm Mildred Noftall."

"We don't live far," Maddie explained. "My brother's working on a Heritage Fair project about our family's past."

"And your family is?"

"We're the Rae family," Maddie said. Gwyn liked the pride in her voice.

The woman's plain face broke into a remarkably pretty smile. "Oh, the Rae papers. I accessioned them myself." She must have noticed Gwyn's puzzlement because she added, "Organized the papers and assigned their numbers. It's a wonderful collection, but it's not here."

"It must be," Maddie replied. "My father said everything was deposited in the Provincial Archives after my grandmother died."

"They are in the Provincial Archives," the woman explained. "Just not here. You'll have to go to the Mews Annex." She sighed. "I wish we could get that collection over here."

"Why can't you?" Maddie asked.

"Dr. Hart Mews refused to move here when The Rooms opened." The woman lowered her voice to a whisper, even though the room was empty. "The Fort Townsend debacle, you know. He can't forgive the province for failing to preserve the site. Everyone else has forgotten by now. Unfortunately, Dr. Mews is not like everyone else." Her voice returned to normal. "So he's still in the old Colonial Building where the archives used to be. In the basement, all alone now, with papers he has grown too fond of to part with. He will be pleased to see you."

"Is that office open on Sundays?" Maddie asked.

The woman looked scandalized. "Heavens no. Monday to Friday, afternoons only, and you'll need an appointment."

Gwyn felt his heart sink. This was going to take forever.

"Not much demand for the papers in the Mews Annex, though," she continued. "I should be able to book you in tomorrow. Let me check." She led them over to a desk, where she extracted an old-fashioned ledger book. "Yes, Monday afternoon is fine." She peered at them over her reading glasses. "Three-thirty?"

"Could you make it four?" Maddie asked. "I have soccer practice," she explained to Gwyn as the woman wrote down the appointment. "You can come watch and then we'll walk over together."

When they left the room a few minutes later, Maddie said, "That wasn't so hard. You don't even have to work here."

"It's not such a bad place," Gwyn admitted. They turned to a wall of glass that faced the harbour. "Wow. You can see right out through the Narrows." Now that he knew he wouldn't have to come here again, Gwyn realized he wouldn't have minded.

Maddie pointed down, across to the street below. "Look, there's the Kirk, Daniel's church." It was a red-brick building with slate tiles on the roof, small for a church, its tall, thin steeple capped with green copper. "Come on," Maddie said. "I paid admission so we could look around. Let's find the natural history exhibit."

Gwyn smiled. She'd chosen the one she knew he'd like best.

Inside, Gwyn was stopped by the sight of a familiar glass case. "The great auk. They moved it from the university?"

"I think they brought it here when The Rooms opened."

Gwyn read the card inside. "On loan from the Centre for Newfoundland Studies." He looked at the carefully arranged collection of bleached bones. "You know, Dad took me into the Centre for Newfoundland Studies when I was only five or six and showed me this. Then he explained what the word 'extinct' meant. I never forgot. The idea that something could disappear forever just blew me away."

"What about the dinosaurs?" Maddie asked.

"This mattered more to me, I think, because it was caused by people. And dinosaurs aren't exactly extinct. Birds are descended from the same line as *Tyrannosaurus rex*."

"Right, then the great auk isn't exactly extinct either. We still have murres and razorbills and puffins, all those—what do you call that family?"

"Alcids. Maddie, shut up," Gwyn said. He was smiling, though. Maddie tried to pretend she wasn't interested in birds, but once in a while she'd let something like this slip so Gwyn knew the things he cared about really did matter to her.

By the time they left The Rooms, Gwyn was glad he'd finally gone inside.

As soon as they rounded the corner to their block, he noticed the extra car in the driveway. "Oh, Sunny's here for dinner."

"*Fabulous*," Maddie said.

Gwyn's laugh exploded like a sneeze. "Fabulous" was one of Sunny's favourite words, and Maddie had a perfect ear for voices. She'd summed up exactly how they felt about Sunny without saying one unkind thing. This was his Maddie. Whatever had been troubling her earlier was gone.

The first thing Gwyn saw was when they walked into the house was Sunny's white parka—arctic-weight, down-filled, top of the line in technical clothing, enviable in every way. It was lying on the floor under the coat rack, one corner wicking filthy water from the boot tray.

"Oh me nerves," Maddie said, using their Gran's voice as she lifted the coat and carefully returned it to the rack. Gwyn and Maddie exchanged a glance. *Here we go*, it said, and in they went.

Sunny, who was six feet tall, was overflowing out of Gwyn's chair, a small glass of sherry balanced at the tips of her fingers. "Here they are!" she cried. "Back from The Rooms. Gwynnie, I thought you'd taken a vow of perpetual Rooms-lessness."

Tom spoke before Gwyn could figure out exactly what she'd said. "People can change, Sunny." Anyone else would have read his tone: back off, you're talking to my son. Not Sunny.

"Can they? That's news to me."

It would be. This perfectly logical reply made a mad dash for Gwyn's lips. Though he managed to quash it just in time, the effort drove every other thought from his head and he stood there, literally speechless. Sunny could do that without even trying.

"Gwyn was wondering about the Viking dig, Sunny." His mother came to the rescue, restoring the balance with a single sentence.

"Oh, it was *fabulous*."

Gwyn didn't dare look at Maddie. Instead, he sat down, allowing himself a smile. "Mom said you found things no one had ever seen before?"

"We did. We weren't sure there was anything left to find, and the blackflies were terrible. At least we were near civilization. I'm getting too old to go for days without a hot shower. Imagine working in a trench cut through peat bog, up to our ankles in water most of the time. As bad as picking cranberries. Remember the time we went out to that cranberry bog near Lead Cove, Annie? And you got stuck?"

"I do remember, but you haven't told us what you found."

"Right. Well, we hoped we'd find some wooden artifacts. Wood doesn't rot in peat, you know, and they'd
found some during the dig in the Seventies, a plank and
shavings from woodworking. Nothing like this, though.
We found weaving tablets! Over forty of them. It's a huge
discovery. We've had a big Viking exhibit planned for
this March at The Rooms for ages. Now, we'll be able to
showcase these tablets."

"Weaving tablets, what are they? Part of a loom?"
Annette asked.

"No! With weaving tablets you don't need a loom.
So they travel really well. I knew a bit about them but
I'd never paid attention until we found these. I've been
meeting with local weavers to find someone who wants
to learn how to use them, so we can have demonstrations
at the exhibit. I've got books in the car. Do you want to
see?" Everyone did.

Gwyn heard Sunny curse when she discovered the
damage to her parka, then the door slammed.

"Thanks for picking up my coat, ducklings," she said
as she returned with a cloth bag full of books. "Good
thing it's washable. Here we go." The book she plucked
from her bag was filled with scraps of paper, makeshift
bookmarks. Sunny set it down open on the coffee table
so they could all see. "Have a look." Colourful bands of
weaving sprang from the pages.

"Those patterns look so complicated," Annette said. "How could anyone do that without a loom?"

Sunny flipped backwards in the book and put it down again. The photograph showed a woman sitting with long strands of yarn running from a hook above her to her belt. Sunny pointed to some flat, square pieces of wood strung into the yarn.

"See? These are the tablets, or cards, the Americans call them. They were usually made of wood or leather. Most have four holes but they can have six, or three. One weaving thread goes through each of the holes. As the weaver turns the cards, different sets of threads open and close. The colours of the threads and the way the cards are moved determine the pattern. Because each card can turn in any direction, a good weaver can create really complex patterns."

Maddie picked up the book. "This is so interesting. I'm doing textile arts in school. My teacher said she'd love to teach us to weave but we'd all need looms. I should tell her about this."

Sunny beamed. "It would be great to get a class involved. What's your teacher's name?"

"Ms. Keats. Lucy, I think."

"Oh, yes! The weavers mentioned her to me. I'll give you my card. Tell her about this and ask her to get in touch with me, would you?"

A bell chimed at the back of the house. "Dinner in ten minutes," Annette said, rising from her chair. "Somebody set the table."

Sunny was happy to talk about tablet weaving and her plans for the exhibit at The Rooms while they ate. When she was ready to leave, Gwyn realized he'd actually enjoyed the evening.

"I'm glad Sunny found something to throw herself into," Annette said as the door closed behind her.

"Not many people can dig up a whole new interest like that," Tom joked, then he looked more serious. "It's a welcome change."

o o o o

That night, getting ready for bed, Gwyn remembered the Mews Annex. He didn't look forward to meeting new people often, but he really wanted to meet Dr. Hart Mews.

When he fell asleep, Gwyn dreamed himself into a cluttered room filled with bookcases draped with bands of tablet weaving and glass display cases, every one holding the skeleton of a great auk. Somewhere in the back of the room, someone was roaring. It was Sunny, and, though he couldn't see her, Gwyn knew she was dressed in a Viking costume. A man in an old-fashioned Victorian suit sat at a desk. Gwyn recognized Dr. Hart Mews, even though he looked exactly like Gwyn's father.

"I've lost my dragon," he said. "Can you help me find him?"

CHAPTER FIVE

The Mews Annex

When Gwyn saw Tyler Cull at school on Monday morning, the memory of Friday afternoon returned with a shock. So much had happened over the weekend, Gwyn had forgotten him. But Tyler didn't even seem to see Gwyn as they passed in the hall. That was the way it was with bullies—they'd pretend you didn't exist, then, just when you relaxed, they'd pounce. Gwyn knew this cat-and-mouse game was supposed to unnerve him. Today, he was too busy thinking about the Mews Annex to care. The day seemed to last decades but, finally, school was over.

Maddie's high school was just beside Gwyn's junior high, only a few blocks from their house. Gwyn decided to go home first and dump his backpack. Why did she want him to watch her soccer practice? It wasn't like Maddie to forget how much he hated sports. To him, sports teams were just another way to make people conform. He'd go to a game if it mattered to Maddie but never a practice. Once home, Gwyn let himself fall into a book, ignoring the clock until he was nearly late. He grabbed his coat and rushed out.

As soon as Gwyn entered the gym, he could see something was wrong. Maddie was always calm and happy when she played any sport, in control in a way Gwyn envied in spite of himself. Not today, though. She was red-faced, somehow off balance. Gwyn slid onto a bench and watched to see if he could figure out what was wrong. It didn't take long.

The girls had been divided into practice teams. When Maddie got the ball, a teammate put a foot out to trip her when the coach wasn't watching—a *teammate*! None of the other girls reacted, not even the one who was supposed to be reffing, as if tripping Maddie were perfectly normal. The girl who'd tripped her was short, but with that hair and makeup, she could have passed for an adult. Her smirk made Gwyn's hands form themselves into fists before he knew what he was doing. He looked down, appalled, and forced his fingers open.

Maddie looked like she wanted to kill someone. A few minutes later, when the ball came her way, she headed it with deadly precision into the face of the girl who'd tripped her. The place exploded. The ref's whistle blasted. The coach hurled herself off the bench, wading through the girls crowding around Maddie's victim. Through the push of bodies, Gwyn could see the girl clutching her nose with both hands, doubled over with pain. Maddie was close to tears and, though she stood alone in the middle of the gym, she reminded Gwyn of a cornered animal. He could only sit and watch.

Maddie just stood panting with her hands clenched until the other girl looked okay. Finally, the coach turned to her. "Rae, you're out of the game. Just leave. Learn to control your aggression, or you'll be off the team."

Maddie turned on her heel and left without a word. Gwyn waited for play to resume so he could slip out unnoticed. As he left, he took a good look at the girl Maddie had hit. She was on the bench, surrounded by friends. Another girl said something and she laughed. She didn't look like she'd been hurt at all.

Maddie came out a few minutes later, walking so fast Gwyn almost had to run to keep up with her. The sky was a solid ceiling of grey, the damp wind sharp and steady. Gwyn pulled up his hood. The city never cleared sidewalks in winter. They had to walk between the ploughed snowbanks and the traffic, single file. Maddie went ahead, not talking, so Gwyn had to figure out a way to start.

"What did the coach mean? You're not aggressive."

Maddie slowed a little. "She only sees my reactions," she called over her shoulder. "The other girls are good at hiding what they do. When Megan was captain, they were more careful. Today was the worst ever."

Gwyn remembered how upset Maddie had been when she talked about Megan leaving. "So, this has been going on for a while?"

"Months. That girl who tripped me, Jasmine O'Connor, manipulates everyone. The girls, anyway." Her words rushed out in a torrent. "Good grades aren't cool, she says." Maddie snorted. "As if she could get them. She says everyone has to get under 60 percent in everything except gym."

"That's ridiculous," Gwyn said. Then he remembered his last report card and blushed, glad that Maddie couldn't see him.

"It's stupid," Maddie agreed, "and I'm not going to do it. She says cool girls have to have boyfriends too. So all these girls are doing everything they can to get the attention of guys they don't even like, just to be cool. She talks non-stop about Eric Larsen and how he's going to ask her out any day now."

"Bunny's big brother?" Gwyn asked. He'd known Bunny since grade one.

Maddie laughed. "You still call her Bunny?"

"Everyone does. Bunny's okay. When we were in grade four, Robbie Clough's father had no job for a while and they had to use food banks. Bunny used to bring food from home and sneak it into his backpack when she thought we weren't looking. Nobody ever makes fun of Bunny."

Maddie nodded. "Eric seems like good guy too. He's captain of the school hockey team and plays bass guitar in his own band. Just like Bunny, everyone likes him. It'll be a shame if Jasmine gets her hooks into him." She shook her head. "Gwyn, I don't want a boyfriend yet and I'm not going to let anyone bully me into something I'm not ready for."

A spate of traffic made conversation impossible. Gwyn tried to take it all in. Maddie unpopular. Maddie bullied. The world had just turned upside down. After a few blocks, they turned onto a side street where they could finally walk side by side.

"How does she even know your grades?" Gwyn asked.

"Sometimes the teachers announce who got the highest marks when they give papers back. There are lots of grade ten girls who want Jasmine to like them so they tell her things. And I made the honour roll. That's pretty obvious. Jasmine knows I'm not playing along and she thinks she's got to break me. The worst part is the way the teacher thinks I'm the bully."

Gwyn had heard enough. "This is wrong. I'm telling."

"Gwyn! After all the secrets I've kept for you!"

Gwyn knew he owed her his silence. "You're right."

"Anyway, can you imagine Mom wading into this?" Maddie continued. "She'd make things ten times worse."

"You wanted me to know, didn't you? That's why you asked me to see your practice today."

"I didn't expect anything like that to happen, but yes. I had to tell someone."

Gwyn didn't know whether to be pleased or appalled. "What about your friends?" He always pictured Maddie surrounded by friends.

"Half of them went to Prince of Wales when we started high school in the fall, and the ones who are here are terrified of being unpopular." Maddie made a face. "They don't even talk to me now. I'm in this alone."

"Not any more, you aren't." Gwyn spoke without thinking, then realized how foolish this must sound, coming from him. "I mean, I guess I can't do much. Whatever I can do, I will," he finished awkwardly.

Maddie didn't laugh, she looked grateful. She'd never looked at Gwyn that way before. She wasn't supposed to, either, so he changed the subject as they approached Bannerman Park.

"Do we know where we're supposed to go in the Colonial Building?"

"Mrs. Noftall said the basement. Let's get off the street." Dog-walkers had already made paths through the new snow in the park.

The Colonial Building had once been the home of the colonial legislature, and it bit into a corner of Bannerman Park. Gwyn remembered there had been riots there in the 1930s; he'd seen a photograph in one of his textbooks of this building with all the windows shattered. Except for the windows, it hadn't changed since then — a large, grey-stone block that made Gwyn think of the word "edifice." The front had a towering row of stone columns resting on a massive staircase that went all the way up to the second storey. It seemed more approachable from the side.

"It's not the basement at all," Maddie said, peering through the window in a wooden door, "just the ground floor. I guess we'll have to walk to the front and go through some kind of security." She tried the door. "It's not locked!" She raised her eyebrows. "Should we go in?"

"That's what we're here for," Gwyn replied. "They can chase us upstairs if they want."

The hall had an arched plaster ceiling that would have looked graceful if the space hadn't been crammed with pipes and ugly fluorescent lights. "It sure looks like a basement," Gwyn said. They found a door with a sign, neatly hand-lettered in black ink. Gwyn read it out loud, but quietly. Something about this place made him want to whisper. "*Mews Annex, Provincial Archives, Dr. Hart Mews, Archivist Emeritus.*" He had to sound the last word out.

"What do you suppose 'emeritus' means?" Maddie asked.

Gwyn shrugged. "Maybe he has special merits."

Maddie giggled. "What, like archive badges?" She'd gone through Sparks and Brownies and Guides, collecting merit badges all the way. Gwyn had quit Beavers.

"Sure. On a sash he wears for special occasions." Gwyn warmed to the idea. "A little gold filing cabinet for putting things away properly. One of those funny machines . . ."

"A microfilm reader," Maddie supplied. "And a badge for making neat labels." She took a deep breath to stop laughing. "We should knock."

As she spoke, the door swung open. "I thought I heard someone." The voice was dry and brittle as old paper.

Dr. Hart Mews looked impossibly ancient. He might have been tall once, but now he was almost the same height as Gwyn. His hair was white and straight as thistledown, but his pale-blue eyes looked younger than the rest of him.

"You must be the Rae children. They told me you were coming. I don't particularly care for children, might as well tell you that right off. Most seem sullen nowadays. Angry. Prone to random acts of violence. The news is full of it." He peered intently at Maddie's face, then at Gwyn's. They were still smiling from the archive jokes. "At least you *seem* cheerful." He sounded as if he thought this might be some kind of trick. He opened the door wide with unexpected energy and, before they could react, said, "Well, what are you waiting for? Come in." He walked away and they followed him into the Mews Annex.

The room had high ceilings, and the wood-framed windows were as big as doors. Rows of wooden bookcases made it difficult to guess how big the room was. There were no cases of great auk skeletons, but otherwise it was eerily close to Gwyn's dream. Every flat surface, whether table, desk or cabinet, overflowed with books and papers. Two desks facing each other were stacked with tall, narrow boxes, all a gloomy sort of grey.

"I pulled the Rae papers. They're on the desks by the windows." Dr. Mews had disappeared somewhere into the bookcases, but his voice was clear. "Use the gloves."

Gwyn wondered what that meant until he looked at the desks and saw two pairs of flimsy cotton gloves. The tiny gloves expanded as he pulled them on. He wiggled his fingers at Maddie.

"What do these gloves do?" she called out over the bookcases.

"They protect the materials from the salts and oils on your hands."

Maddie put her gloves on too. "Where do we start?" she whispered.

"The papers were accessioned by type in chronological order." Though Dr. Mews was old, there was nothing wrong with his hearing. "There's a finding aid in the first box."

Maddie looked at Gwyn and shrugged. He knew she wondered what a finding aid was but didn't want to ask again. He studied the labels and pulled out the box with the lowest number. Inside, along with file folders, they found a booklet bound in green cardboard. Gwyn read the label. *"Finding Aid, Rae Collection, Boxes FN5568 to FN5598."*

"Wow," Maddie said. "Thirty-one boxes."

"Thirty and a half, actually. I only pulled the first half dozen or so," Dr. Mews said, reappearing. "You won't get that far today. It's nice to look ahead sometimes, though." Gwyn heard his voice soften as Dr. Mews looked at the boxes with the kind of affection most people save for children or pets.

"When I find something interesting, can I take a box home?" Gwyn asked.

Dr. Mews drew back as if Gwyn had slapped him. "Good heavens, no. An archive is not a lending library. These papers are the property of the government. You may take notes. With pencils only, no pens." He paused, then asked, "Why are you doing this? You seem too young to be interested in family history."

"It's a Heritage Fair project," Gwyn and Maddie said together, then they laughed.

"Oh, the Heritage Fair. I've been a judge a few times. Then you may want some papers or photographs copied for display. That can be arranged. You probably know there's an extensive collection of photographs. They're stored separately but they're listed in the finding aid. I suggest you look at the papers first. That way, when you see the photos, you'll have a better idea what you're looking at."

Maddie pulled up a chair and sat down. It took her two tries to open the finding aid. Gwyn picked up a pencil and was amazed to find thin cotton gloves could make his fingers so clumsy.

"Four boxes of sermons and notes for sermons," Maddie said, paging down through the finding aid. "How many boxes of correspondence?" She counted silently. "Six!"

"I guess they wrote letters the way we write e-mail," Gwyn said. He looked over her shoulder. "'Letters from James and Agatha Rae.' From Agatha and her husband!" The thought of reading letters from their great-great-grandparents sent a shiver right down his spine.

"Wow," Maddie said, turning a page. "The journals and natural history notebook start in 1862, way before he came here. He must have been young then, about your age, maybe. This is odd," she continued. "It says the note-book labelled 'D' has big blank sections."

"I wonder why," Gwyn said. His eyes skipped across to the next page and something else caught his attention. "Look, there are public lectures." He read a title, "'One Creation or Many?' I wonder what that means?" It was all wonderfully bewildering, like Christmas morning.

They were still reading the finding aid when Dr. Mews reappeared. "I'm closing up now."

Gwyn looked out the window. Night had fallen. At least an hour must have passed. "We didn't even get to the files. Can I come back tomorrow?"

Dr. Mews almost smiled. "Certainly. Any afternoon. It's a daunting collection. I half expected you to have one look and never return. Here are the copying costs." He handed Gwyn a sheet of paper.

Gwyn thought about the work ahead of him, all the reading, the decisions, writing the essays and designing a display. It seemed as if he might drown in a sea of paper. Maddie must have felt the same way because they both sat at the table without moving.

"Off you go," Dr. Mews said. "Shoo." As if they were chickens. They were still pulling on their jackets when he closed the door on them.

Maddie giggled. "He's certainly not what I expected," she said as they stepped outside.

"He's not," Gwyn agreed, "and this project is going to be a lot of work."

"You're sure you want to do it? You know you don't have to."

Gwyn was surprised she'd give him a choice, and his answer surprised him too. "Sure. It's more interesting than anything else I've done for school this year."

"I'd like to read the journals," Maddie said. "I mean, how often to you get to read someone else's private thoughts? And if I find anything interesting, I'll let you know."

"That would be great. I can't wait to tell Dad about this."

"And you won't tell him anything else, will you?"

Gwyn shook his head. "You can trust me."

The damp wind that had hounded them on the walk from school was gone. Each street lamp cast a golden halo on the snowy park. Life is good, Gwyn thought.

o o o o

At home, a surprise was waiting. "I remembered that tin of Daniel's," Tom said. "It's on the dining-room table. I'll pick you up after school tomorrow so you can get those newspaper articles. Now, I've got to get supper going. You go ahead and have a look."

Gwyn found an old tin biscuit box with chipped paint and patches of rust, decorated with a false mosaic pattern of bluebirds and daffodils.

"Open it," Maddie urged.

Inside was what their Gran would have called odd-ments: useless things no one had the heart to throw away. Gwyn took out several skeins of cotton thread, a rosette of red, white and blue ribbon and a ring of rough black cloth.

"That's an armband," Maddie said, taking it from him. "Men used to wear those when someone died."

There was a pincushion in the shape of tartan bag-pipes, badly faded but still holding some rusty straight pins, and a collection of shell buttons in assorted sizes. At the bottom of the box sat a large, black, cast-iron key. The skin on Gwyn's scalp prickled. It looked exactly like the giant key in his dream. He grabbed it, then backed away with a cry as it clattered back into the tin.

"What's wrong?" Maddie asked.

"It, it—tingled, like it had an electrical current run-ning through it."

When Maddie picked it up, her mouth made a per-fect O. "You're right. It's a sort of buzz. It doesn't hurt though."

"I know, it just surprised me." He took the key from Maddie, gingerly. The tingle seemed weaker, but it was still there.

"Can somebody set the table?" their father called from the kitchen.

Gwyn put the key back and closed the lid of the biscuit tin over it. "The tin is metal," he said. "Maybe the key built up some kind of electrical charge while it was in there." He needed a logical explanation, even if he didn't believe it.

All through supper, Gwyn and Maddie told their parents about their adventure in the archives. That was how Gwyn thought of it now, an adventure.

"There are all these public lectures too," Gwyn said near the end of the meal. "What's the difference between a sermon and a public lecture?"

"Public lectures weren't religious," his father replied. "They were just for fun."

"People went to lectures for fun?" Maddie asked.

"Yes. They didn't have the Internet or TV, not even the radio."

Gwyn remembered something. "The title I read sounded religious. It was 'One Creation or Many?'"

His father put down his fork. "So Daniel was interested in evolution. That's fascinating. I took a history of science course when I was an undergrad and we spent a lot of time on the Victorian period. It was such a great time. All these clues had been lying around for eons and suddenly they began to fly together. Once people understood geology, they realized the earth was much, much older than anyone had guessed. Then, fossils began to make sense. They could see that animals had changed, but they didn't know how. And, of course, they were trying to reconcile all this with their religion. If animals changed over huge periods of time, how could God have made them in seven days? Some people thought a divine being created creatures at the beginning of the earth then recreated them again when things changed."

"That's pretty goofy," Gwyn said.

"No it isn't. It's easy for us to think so today, now that we have more answers. In fact, you have to come up with a lot of ideas before you get the right one. That's science. Darwin rejected the idea of successive creation but it made sense at the time. Perfectly good scientists believed dinosaurs were animals that didn't get onto Noah's ark. As a clergyman, Daniel would have had a natural interest in creation and evolution."

"Is that why he kept all those notebooks about natural history?" Maddie asked.

"Natural history was a popular hobby in the 1800s," her father replied. "People collected moths and beetles, fossils and flowers the way some people play with computer programs and hardware today." He smiled. "Victorian geeks were armed with butterfly nets. I wish I'd known about those notebooks when I was doing that history of science course. I'm sure they'd have given me a great essay topic. Everything just sat in boxes for years until my mother finally opened them."

"Do you think that would be a good idea for my Heritage Fair project?" Gwyn asked. "I was going to tell the story of the shipwreck and how Daniel died, but there's so much stuff in the archives. Maybe natural history is more interesting."

"More cheerful, that's for sure," Maddie said.

Tom smiled. "More sophisticated, too. I'm sure you'll find your project in those notebooks. We can look for some books about Victorians and natural history in the university library when we go tomorrow. Was there anything in that box I brought home?"

"I'd better show you." Gwyn got the box and placed the key in his father's hand.

"Strange. Almost like an electrical current. That's not possible, though. How unusual. Take it, Annie." Tom handed the key to his wife.

She turned it on her palm. "It's nice," she said, "but there's nothing strange about it."

"You don't feel anything?" Gwyn could hardly believe it.

"Maybe it's one of those things some people experience and others don't," Tom said.

"Like being a supertaster?" Gwyn asked.

Maddie groaned. "You had to bring that up?"

Annette suddenly looked as if she'd turned to stone.

Gwyn winced. He'd forgotten how upset his mother had been that Sunday a few years ago when they'd all gone into Tom's lab for a fun-with-genetics outing. Tom had given them papers soaked with a special chemical to put on their tongues. He, Maddie and Gwyn had convulsed with the bitter taste—they were supertasters, people with extra taste buds who experience flavours more intensely. But to Annette Prothero, the nutritionist, the paper had no taste at all. She was not a supertaster. Though she'd tried to pretend it didn't matter, the day had been ruined for all of them. And no one had mentioned it again, until now.

Tom reached across the table, took the key from his wife and held it for a moment. "You're right," he said, "There's nothing strange about this key. Whatever it was is gone." He handed it to Gwyn with a look that said *Put it away.* He should have wanted to spend hours trying to understand what made the key so strange.

It still tingled in Gwyn's hand, and he promised himself one thing. That key had once unlocked a door, maybe not in The Rooms, but somewhere. If the door was still around, Gwyn would find it.

CHAPTER SIX

THE "D" NOTEBOOK

G wyn and his father found books about Victorians and natural history in the university library, and then, in the basement, Tom showed Gwyn how to use a microfilm reader so they could find the old newspaper articles about the shipwreck and Daniel Rae. The obituaries were a surprise.

"I always knew Daniel was a highly respected member of the community," Tom said at dinner that night. "Turns out he was a bit of an oddball, too."

"Really?" Annette said. "An oddball clergyman? I'm surprised."

"Go ahead, Gwyn, read what you found."

Gwyn got the photocopies and spread them out on the table. "'The Reverend Daniel Rae will be missed for his brilliant sermons and the compassion he showed to the poor,'" he read, "'And those who knew him best will also miss his eccentric sense of humour, for Mr. Rae could often be overheard talking to himself, and even referring to himself as a hermit . . .'"

"See?" Tom said. "That's not the way I imagined him at all."

Annette turned to Gwyn. "I wonder if you'll get the same impression from his papers."

He smiled. "Me too."

Eager to understand Daniel now, Gwyn went straight to the Mews Annex every day after school. Maddie joined him a few times a week. They didn't talk about her troubles, but Gwyn guessed the family papers gave Maddie the same kind of escape he found. It was as if they'd discovered a door into the past that they could disappear into, away from all the bullies. Together, they looked through Daniel's brittle, faded collections of dried seaweed, ferns and flowers, all carefully dated and labelled, plants that seemed like they'd dissolve into to dust if anyone breathed on them. Then Gwyn settled down to the natural history notebooks while Maddie read the journals. She also asked for the files of photographs, which came on something Dr. Mews called "contact sheets," old-fashioned pages of prints with many small copies of photos on each. In his one formal portrait, Daniel Rae was unmistakably related to Gwyn's father: tall, dark-haired and serious-looking in his stiff Victorian clothes but with a twinkle in his eye. "We'll get that enlarged for your project," Maddie said, copying the accession number onto an order form.

As they walked home, Maddie told Gwyn what she'd read in the journals about Daniel's distress at the poverty he saw in St. John's and his delight to find he could walk from the city into the countryside. "He doesn't sound odd at all," she concluded. Daniel began to seem like a friend Gwyn and Maddie never saw.

In the evenings, Gwyn worked through the books from the university library on natural history and ideas about evolution in Victorian Britain. They weren't hard to read, and all the stuff he was learning began to seep into his dreams. One night, he saw a seashore where men in tweed suits and women with long, bell-shaped skirts dipped into tidal pools and exclaimed over their treasures, their voices high and thin under the vastness of a pure blue sky. Above them, creatures nothing like birds swooped and soared. The dragons were so at home in this dream world, no one paid any attention. Gwyn breathed the salt air, felt the breeze on his face and woke up relaxed, as if he'd been on vacation.

The next day, as he and Maddie walked home from the Colonial Building, Gwyn noticed that the sky wasn't as dark as it had been a few weeks before. Even though February never seemed like the shortest month, it was passing. "There's something strange in the journals," Maddie told him. "Daniel's always talking about 'H,' but I can't figure out if it's a person or a pet. Just when I'm sure it's a pet, he says something that makes it sound like a person."

"People talk about their pets as if they're people all the time."

"I'm not sure they did a hundred years ago," Maddie replied. "Maybe this is why they thought Daniel was odd. Do you want to have a look?"

Gwyn sighed. "I've got to keep reading. I still need a topic for the Heritage Fair. I'm getting worried. The natural history notebooks are just a mishmash. I guess I was expecting Daniel to be a real scientist, more like Dad."

Maddie frowned. "That's too bad. You could always go back to the story about the shipwreck, couldn't you?"

"I guess. I just hate to think I did all this reading for nothing. I'll stick at it awhile longer."

The next afternoon, working alone, Gwyn opened the "D" notebook. He remembered Maddie saying something about this one when they'd first come to the Mews Annex, but he didn't know what. That was okay. He'd find out if it was important.

On the first page, Daniel had written a quotation, all by itself. It was so odd that Gwyn read it aloud to see if his ears could make more sense of it than his eyes had.

"*'I am a brother to dragons, and a companion to owls*. Job 30:29.'"

"Not job. *Job*. Rhymes with *globe*. Don't young people learn anything these days?" Dr. Mews had appeared from nowhere and he was frowning. "It's from the Bible. The Book of Job."

"Oh, when things went wrong Gran used to say, 'This is just like the Book of Job.'" Gwyn replied. "What does this mean?"

"Generally, when people quote from the Book of Job, it's because they feel burdened." Dr. Mews shook his head. "That is an odd one, though. I'd certainly never noticed it before."

Gwyn settled down to read the "D" notebook. Right away, he saw it was different. Everything was related to a single topic: flight and the nature of flying animals. There were diagrams, topic headings, even a few newspaper clippings. The book began with a list of every sort of flying animal Daniel knew of: birds, bats, different insects, even flying fish. Then, there was a question: "*Why do different types of animals take to the air?*" with Daniel's answers. "*1. Increased speed,*" he had written, "*1 b) access to prey. I have noticed birds chasing insects in the air. Without wings, they would not be fast enough to catch them. The same is true of terns and kittywakes who chase fish.*"

Gwyn's heart began to pound. He'd hit pay dirt. Here,

finally, was a logical investigation he could build a project around. It even involved birds! By the time the annex closed, he knew he had the topic for his Heritage Fair project.

The next time Maddie came with him, she said, "Maybe I'll make notes about 'H' and you'll see what I mean."

"Sure," Gwyn replied, only half listening. Maddie's interest in Daniel's pet hardly seemed to matter now.

Today, Gwyn studied the diagrams of wings. Daniel wasn't a bad artist. There was a sketch of a bird's wing with feathers, then just the bones, and a second set of sketches looked like bats' wings. There was a third kind of wing, only the exterior, no skeleton, and Gwyn didn't recognize it at all. This featherless web of skin wasn't reinforced by four elongated finger bones as the bats' wings were. The bone structure looked more like a bird's wing, but not quite. Three fingers were bunched together at the joint where the fourth finger had evolved into an elongated wing bone. They were not the fused, vestigial fingers of a bird, though. Instead, they stood out from the joint of the wing in what appeared to be a small, functioning, three-toed paw. Gwyn sat back, puzzled. What had wings like that? Nothing living in Newfoundland, for sure. Maybe Daniel was imagining things? Making up an animal?

Gwyn read on. At first, the text just described the diagrams; there was nothing to say what the strange wing sketch might represent. Then Daniel began to describe an animal in flight: "*H lifts off from his powerful legs and launches himself into the air like a missile. It is amazing to see. The wings spring open with a rippling noise that recalls to me the wind in canvas sails and propel him upward in just a few strong strokes. H is quite expert at catching rising currents of warm air and circles upward, ever upward, flapping now only to propel himself higher. And then he soars, majestic lord of the air. The birds (who can perceive him) are sometimes disturbed by this strange intruder.*"

Though it sounded as if Daniel was describing something he'd actually seen, he must have imagined it. Maddie would want to know Gwyn had found something about "H." He started to speak but stopped when he saw her face. Tears streamed down her cheeks. She was holding the journal out so it didn't get splashed.

"What's wrong?" Gwyn asked.

Maddie looked stricken as she sniffed loudly. "Daniel just found out his brother James died. It happened so quickly. He caught a cold or something and it got worse, went into his lungs and he died. Letters moved so slowly in those days, Daniel didn't even know James was sick. By the time he got the letter, his younger brother had been dead for weeks. He's heartbroken." She sounded as if she were talking about a friend. "Listen." She searched back across a page and began to read. "'*I can hardly bring myself to accept the news. Part of me believes he is still safe in Aberdeen with his young wife. When I think I shall never look upon his face again in this life, or hear his voice, never joke with him, never share a day of trekking in the wilds, or later, sit by the fire with him, resting our weary bones and sharing our stories, my heart is so full of grief, it seems ready to burst. How am I to bear this pain?*'" Maddie's voice faltered on the last line. She gave a shaky sigh. "Here's the part that really got me. '*I must provide for Agatha, his bride but a year ago, his widow now, lest she sink into poverty after the child is born.*' Oh, Gwyn," Maddie wailed, "she was *pregnant* when her husband died."

Dr. Mews appeared, placing a box of tissues on the desk in front of Maddie. "Family tragedy?" he asked. Gwyn frowned. If he was making fun of Maddie, Gwyn would have something to say. There was genuine concern in those pale-blue eyes, though, so Gwyn relaxed and explained while Maddie blew her nose.

Dr. Mews actually patted Maddie's shoulder. "These stories can be very affecting. You're certainly not the first to sit and cry in the archives, my dear. So, Hamish Rae was a posthumous child. Fascinating."

"What does that mean?" The tip of her nose was still red but Maddie had stopped crying.

"Born after his father died," Dr. Mews explained. "It used to happen more often, of course, before modern

medicine. Here's the interesting part: there's an old super-
stition that goes with it. People used to believe a posthumous child would have special healing powers."

"Oh!" Maddie said.

Dr. Mews smiled and nodded. "Indeed. Hamish Rae
became a very fine doctor. I remember him well. So the
story does have a happy ending, even if both the broth-
ers, James and Daniel, died young. Hamish lived a long
and happy life, and here you are, his great-grandchildren.
And none of them forgotten. Perhaps that is all that the
dead can ask, to be kept alive in our memories." He spoke
of "the dead" in such a friendly way. Gwyn realized that
most of the people this man had known were already
gone. How lonely would that be?

"Well," Dr. Mews said, "enough idle chatter. I have
work to do." The grumpy old man was back again, but at
least Gwyn understood him better. Dr. Mews glanced at
Gwyn's desk. "Ah, you're reading that very odd notebook
with the blank spaces. I remember how curious everyone found it when the collection was accessioned. Paper
was quite valuable in those days. Why on earth would
Daniel Rae leave random parts of his notebook blank? Of
course, it's the same with the journals to a lesser degree."
He turned to Maddie. "You've noticed, I'm sure. I remember wondering if he had some sort of psychological dis-
order that caused him to leave those spaces. Obsessive

compulsive behaviour? It's one of those mysteries about the past we'll never unravel." He was still talking as he walked away.

Maddie raised an eyebrow. Gwyn shrugged and passed the "D" notebook across the desk so she could see it. Every page was covered in Daniel's graceful script. Even the margins had notes on some pages.

There were no blank spaces.

CHAPTER SEVEN

THE KEY

About an hour later, Gwyn and Maddie hurried out of the Mews Annex into a weak winter twilight. They'd worked until the archive closed as usual, saying nothing even though Gwyn was bursting to talk. What else could they do? Dr. Mews had ears like a rabbit.

"That's the second time that's happened!" Maddie said.

"What do you mean?"

"It's the second time we've been able to see, well, not just see—let's say *experience* something that someone else couldn't."

"You mean the key?"

"Yes. Mom couldn't feel what the key was doing—"

"Dad did," Gwyn interrupted. "Then he pretended he didn't to keep Mom from feeling bad."

Maddie swatted this away. "Okay, yes. Dad did. But

Mom couldn't, and Dr. Mews can't see some of Daniel's writing."

"Not just Dr. Mews. He said everyone found it odd. That must mean everyone working in the archives when the papers first came in."

Maddie nodded. "That was before The Rooms opened, when they all worked together, so it's just us . . ."

"And Dad," Gwyn added.

"All right, and Dad," Maddie agreed impatiently. "But why? What's the difference between us and them?"

"Well," Gwyn said slowly, "we're related to Daniel."

"Mom is too."

"Only by marriage. Not biologically."

Maddie stared at him. "You think this is genetic? That's crazy."

"I know. It's crazy. Maybe it's . . ." Gwyn couldn't bring himself to finish.

"Magic?" Maddie breathed the missing word into the cold air between them. It hovered for an instant like some impossible creature come to life, then vanished.

Though she wasn't teasing, Gwyn could only answer as if she were. "I know. There is no magic. I wish we could set up an experiment to see if there's anyone else like us."

"Are you kidding? You saw how Mom felt when she was left out. And what are we going to do, bring people into the annex under Dr. Mews's nose to ask if they see things he can't?"

"You're right, that wouldn't work."

They walked the rest of the way home in puzzled silence. Just before they reached their house, Maddie sighed. "I don't know about this funny stuff but I really want to get to the end of the journals. It's so sad but I can't stop reading. There's only about a year left. I'll start coming with you more often."

"What about soccer?" The words were out before Gwyn could stop himself.

"I don't think anyone will care if I skip practice. There are only a few games left, and Coach leaves me on the bench most of the time anyway. That works too. The other girls are still mean, but if I'm not playing, I don't react. How are things with you?"

Gwyn shook his head. "It's strange. Tyler Cull seems to have forgotten about me."

"Huh. Maybe he found someone else to pick on. Well, at least no one's throwing your gym shoes away." Maddie stopped abruptly. "I didn't mean to tell you that."

"You're sure you don't want to talk to Mom and Dad about this?"

Maddie shook her head. "Jasmine's loathsome but she's graduating this year. If I can stick it out for four more months, it'll get better." But she didn't sound as if she believed it.

That night, Gwyn fetched the old biscuit tin from the dining room. The key still tingled when he picked it up, and Gwyn realized he didn't need the "D" notebook to conduct an experiment. Before he went upstairs, he slipped the key into his winter jacket.

He said nothing to Maddie about his plan as they walked to school together the next morning, but the key buzzed all the way, through the thin nylon of his jacket's inside pocket, right through the heavy denim of his jeans, like a high-pitched current of anxiety. Approaching school, Gwyn realized the feeling wasn't just coming from the key. How was he going to pull this off?

Think like a scientist, he told himself, and the idea steadied him. Here he was, in the field, looking for the right group of subjects to help him test out his hypothesis. The hypothesis being? a voice inside asked, but he pushed it away. He couldn't afford to be distracted now.

A group of kids shivered by the door. Subjects suffering from nicotine withdrawal, Gwyn thought. Too cranky. The next group had girls in it, and girls were only nice to Gwyn if they knew he was Maddie's brother. He had no way to defend himself against their weird cruelty.

At least a guy like Tyler Cull would punch you and get it over with.

As if this thought had conjured him, there was Tyler Cull, dead ahead. Gwyn veered and found himself facing some boys from his own grade. Two of them, Bryan Morgan and Liam Gosse, had been in Gwyn's classes, off and on, since kindergarten. Suitable subjects.

Giving himself no time to hesitate, Gwyn pulled the key from his pocket. "Ah, hi," he faltered, aware he was blushing. Great start. He pushed his mittened hand into the centre of the group, the key set out like a snack on a tray, trying to think of something to say.

"What's that?" Bryan asked. He was okay. He'd even invited Gwyn to a few of his birthday parties.

"A key!" Gwyn seized the opportunity with such enthusiasm, the others stared at him.

"Yeah, so?" This was Liam, someone Gwyn had always thought of as a bully-in-waiting. The challenge in his voice snapped Gwyn back to his mission.

"So, it belonged to my great-great-uncle, who died in a shipwreck in the 1800s."

"What does it unlock?" Bryan asked, taking the key with his thick ski mitten.

"That's what I'd like to know," Gwyn improvised. "What do you think a key like this would unlock?" He watched, but Bryan seemed unaffected. Could his mitten be too thick?

"Duh. A door? Gimme that." Grant Walsh slipped off this mitten and grabbed the key. No reaction as he turned it in his hand. "Just a key." He was giving it back to Gwyn when Tyler Cull suddenly elbowed his way into the group. The other boys took a step back, an unspoken admission of fear. Everyone except Gwyn, who was too horrified to move.

"What's that?" Tyler lunged, his knuckles red-meat raw from the cold as they closed around the key. "Wha!" The key flew into the air. It bounced off a patch of grey ice, landing at Gwyn's feet, and he bent to snatch it up, not thinking of danger until his nose was directly in front of Tyler's boots. Then he heard the sound that would save him — Liam chuckled.

"That's it, Gosse. You're dead." Liam took off into the crowd. "I'll get you later, Rae." Tyler flung the threat over his shoulder as he disappeared.

"What just happened?" Bryan asked.

"I don't know." Gwyn shoved the key back into his pocket. He knew the other boys were staring as he walked away, but it was the truth. So he and Maddie weren't the only ones who could feel the weirdness of the key . . . but Tyler Cull? That was too strange. Still, the experiment had been a success of sorts, even though Gwyn knew he'd have to watch his back again.

At lunchtime, Gwyn ducked out of school. He left the kitchen tidy so no one would notice he'd been home in the middle of the day and slipped back just after the next bell. He managed to avoid Tyler for the rest of the day, but his last class was biology. Mr. Simms always insisted the lab be cleaned at the end of the day so there was no way to slip out early.

Gwyn expected to find Tyler waiting for him by the lockers, but he was nowhere. Maybe Tyler was still after Liam. Gwyn almost made it to Maddie's school, then he heard Tyler's hoarse voice behind him.

"Wait till I get my hands on you, Rae."

Gwyn was not about to wait. He ran, though Tyler was close and gaining. Just as Tyler grabbed the hood of his coat, Maddie yelled.

"Stop that!" She swept down the hill like some kind of warrior princess. "Get your hands off my brother." Her fury surprised Gwyn. Tyler dropped Gwyn's hood as if it had burned him. Maddie's voice dropped to a malevolent whisper. "If you ever lay another finger on him, I'm going straight to Mr. Snow. Do you understand?" Mr. Snow, the vice-principal, was the ultimate weapon in Gwyn's school. Gwyn could never have complained to him, but as a high-school student, Maddie could. Tyler slunk away without a word, but Gwyn knew the threat alone was not what had scared him off. Maddie had sounded as if she could tear Tyler to pieces with her bare hands. Gwyn guessed a lot of her anger came from her own situation, but he couldn't help being grateful. He said nothing for a few blocks, though, to give her a chance to cool off.

"What was it this time?" she finally asked.

"I did something really stupid." He told her about the key.

He braced for Maddie's anger, but she snorted when he finished. "So much for genetics."

Gwyn was so relieved, he couldn't bring himself to ask what he really wanted to know. Why *had* Tyler reacted to the key?

Maddie sighed. "I'm probably going to finish Daniel's last journal today. It's just like losing a friend."

Gwyn's shoulders sagged as if someone had added a bag of road salt to his backpack. Until this winter, Maddie had never needed friends that didn't exist.

When they reached the Mews Annex, they found Mrs. Noftall waiting for them. "Dr. Mews had a doctor's appointment. He asked me to let you in, said you'd be fine on your own." She bit her lip. "We're just about to open a major exhibit of photographs. I really am needed back at The Rooms. Dr. Mews said he trusted you, though this is highly irregular. I could lose my job if anything were to go wrong."

"We'll be fine," Maddie said. "These papers came from our family to begin with, after all." She pulled on the cotton gloves.

Gwyn copied her, to show how responsible they were. He could hardly believe they'd have a chance to look at Daniel's papers in private. "We won't touch anything else, we promise."

Mrs. Noftall shrugged her coat on. "Your father is Dr. Rae at the university, isn't he? I've heard him on the CBC, talking about genetics. Well, I suppose it's all right. As long as you promise. The door will lock when you leave. I'll be back at five to be sure everything's in order."

Maddie smiled at her, and Gwyn did too. He hoped it was a responsible smile, not a little-kid-about-to-be-left-alone-in-the-candy-store smile, though that was how he felt.

"If anyone else comes by . . ."

"No one ever has," Maddie said, and that was true.

The door clicked shut behind Mrs. Noftall. Maddie and Gwyn were alone in the Mews Annex.

Gwyn knew it was silly to be so delighted, but Maddie's grin told him she felt exactly the same way. "Show me the 'D' notebook again," she demanded.

They paged through it together. "Look, he's writing about 'H' in this book, and 'H' could fly!" Maddie said. "So it *was* some kind of a pet. Huh. I was just about sure he was writing about a person."

"You think he had a pet bird? What, a crow or something?"

"It could have been anything. Sailors brought exotic pets from all over the world. Remember Kathy Furey who moved away in grade six? Her grandmother had a pet monkey when she was little. In a house on Circular Road."

"Well, I don't think 'H' was a flying monkey." Gwyn turned a page to find a newspaper clipping, yellowed and brittle with age. After a few tries, his gloved fingers managed to unfold it. "It's from *The Times* of London."

"What's it about?"

Gwyn read. "The discovery of the fossil of a new 'flying creature' in the Solnhofen Limestone, some place in Germany. Listen to this. It says this was 'another of the pterodactyl group of creatures first described in 1784 by the Italian naturalist Cosmo Alessandro Collini.'" On the page was a note in Daniel's hand: *"How to find out more about these pterodactyl creatures?"* Gwyn got out his notebook. He wrote down "Solnhofen Limestone" and "Cosmo Alessandro Collini." "I'll look these up tonight at home."

Maddie opened the last journal. "I guess I should keep reading."

While they worked in silence, freezing rain began to tap against the windows with needle-sharp claws, frantically scrabbling for their attention, but Gwyn barely registered the noise. The "D" notebook was fascinating. Daniel's ideas about how different flying creatures might be related were faulty, but his intelligence shone through. Gwyn's Heritage Fair project began to fly together. He was almost annoyed when Maddie interrupted.

"Listen. He's writing about 'H' again. *I have booked a passage to Boston so I can meet Agatha and the baby when they arrive. The voyage across the Atlantic alone will be bad enough for them and I am filled with dread for reasons I cannot name. I tell myself this is only because James's death has unsettled me. H is sulking because I will not take him with me. He remembers the voyage from Scotland fondly.'* That makes him sound like a person, doesn't it?" She continued. "*But I will not risk him to such icy weather. With the greatest of reluctance, he has finally consented to stay in the lair at the back of the Kirk. As always, I will put the key in the sewing box, as if it were a thing of little consequence.*'"

Gwyn put the "D" notebook down. "He put the key in the sewing box? The key to—what did he call it?"

"The lair," Maddie said. She looked pale. "The lair at the back of his church."

"What else does it say?" Gwyn prompted.

"Just one more line. Oh my God, Gwyn. Listen. '*Still, I cannot shake this premonition of dread. Anyone who can read this, should I fail to return, will have the right to use that key.*'" She lowered the book to her lap.

"Anyone who can read this. That's us, isn't it?" Gwyn said. "But what did he mean, 'have the right'?"

"I don't know, but anything Daniel left behind would have died a long time ago."

Gwyn shook his head. "The trip to Boston and back would have taken weeks even if nothing had gone wrong. No one would lock a living creature up for weeks and go away. Give it here." Maddie handed the journal over. "See what he wrote?" Gwyn said after a minute. "'*As always, I will put the key in the sewing box.*' This wasn't the first time he'd left it locked up, whatever it was."

"But it doesn't make sense. No wonder people thought Daniel was crazy."

A gust of wind flung ice pellets against the windows. They were streaked with solid, regular lines of ice now, like the bars on a prison. Gwyn reached around his chair, into his jacket pocket. The key's tingle was almost familiar as he put it on the table between them.

"So, the Kirk's right below The Rooms. Are you saying you don't want to find the door this opens?"

Maddie dodged the question, glancing at the windows. "Right now, I say we'd better get home before the weather gets worse."

CHAPTER EIGHT

THE DOOR IN THE KIRK

The freezing rain turned to snow that evening, but Gwyn was at his computer, oblivious. He typed "Solnhofen Limestone" into a search engine and got over a thousand hits, most of them about fossils. Gwyn discovered that the limestone quarries around Solnhofen had revealed fossils long before people knew what fossils were, because the stone was cut into thin sheets for a kind of printing called lithography. There were over six hundred species in the limestone, most of them preserved in amazing detail. Over time, geologists realized that the area had been a shallow lagoon millions of years before, where conditions for fossil-making were just about perfect—no strong currents to carry parts away, with layers of silt gently sifting down upon the dead animals.

He'd been reading for hours when his mother poked her head into his room. "Aren't you going to sleep?"

Gwyn stretched the cramps out of his shoulders, then he glanced at the clock. It was almost midnight. "I was looking up stuff up for the Heritage Fair. Sorry, I lost track of time."

"Time's not all you lost track of. Look outside. Tomorrow should be a snow day." She might as well have said "Tomorrow's Christmas." She laughed. "You could try to look a little less delighted."

Outside, the road and ugly grey snowbanks were hidden by fresh snow. "Pretty."

Annette laughed again. "Most people wouldn't say so. It's supposed to rain overnight and then freeze again. Most of the city should be closed, but I won't take the day off. Hospital patients still have to eat, and if my staff is working, I like to be there. I'm sure the three of you can get along without me."

Gwyn shut down his computer. "I can ask Dad about history of science stuff."

"He's planning to get caught up on some work, but he might have time to talk." She looked like she wanted to say something encouraging about school but caught herself. "Good night, Gwyn," was all she said. Still, she looked happy as she left his room.

Gwyn realized he was happy too. For a long time, his brain had felt blurry, unused. This project was bringing it back into focus. He left the curtains open when he turned off his lamp so soft snow light could fill his room. Most adults seemed to hate winter because of the shovelling and icy roads, but it seemed wrong to hate something that took up so much of every year. He hoped he would never feel that way.

Just before he fell asleep the key drifted into his mind. He and Maddie hadn't been able to talk while they walked home in a hail of flying needles, and their father had already been there when they arrived. After supper, Gwyn couldn't wait to start his computer search, but he knew Maddie. She was too brave and too nosy to let this go. She'd be ready to look for the door that fit the key sooner or later, and Gwyn wasn't about to go looking without her. He could wait.

o o o

By morning, the snow had a glaze like bone china and every tree branch and overhead cable bore a thick casing of ice. When Gwyn came down for breakfast, Maddie was already at the kitchen table. Their father stood by the stove, spatula in hand.

"Pancakes?" he asked.

"Yes, please." Gwyn grinned. Their mother expected them to cook their own breakfasts, but their father still spoiled them sometimes.

"Get a hot breakfast while you can," Tom said. "I won't be surprised if we lose our power. Good thing I can work from hard copy today. I've got a pile of grant applications to review. You two will have to amuse yourselves."

Gwyn avoided Maddie's eyes. "We'll find something to do."

"Good. Maybe you can start by making sure all the flashlights are charged."

When Gwyn's pancakes were made, Tom disappeared into his study. Gwyn knew his father would only come out to make a lunch that he'd eat while he continued to work.

"Help me find the flashlights?" Gwyn asked Maddie.

She nodded. "They're in the basement."

The basement smelled of damp cardboard and laundry detergent. They found a big box labelled "POWER FAILURE" on the shelf above the washing machine and wrestled it down.

"Today would be a good day to check out the Kirk," Gwyn said as they opened the box. "Nobody will be around," he added when Maddie didn't answer.

"Gwyn, this is crazy. People change locks. They clean out rooms. Suppose 'H' is still where Daniel left it. Do you want to find something that's been dead for over a century?"

"Well, it won't be creepy-horror-movie-crawling-with-maggots dead," Gwyn replied. "Something that's been dead for that long will be nicely desiccated."

Maddie smiled in spite of herself. "You make it sound like a package of coconut. I don't know. It seems morbid." On cue, the lights blinked off. They came on again in an instant, but it was a warning.

"What else are we going to do on a day like this?" Gwyn asked. "Maybe a little morbid curiosity is just what we need. Remember what it said in Daniel's journal? We have the right to use the key. It's like we have his permission."

Maddie hesitated, then she nodded. "Okay. Plug in the flashlights to recharge them and I'll tell Dad we're going out."

Gwyn already had his snow pants and winter hiking boots on when she met him in the hall a few minutes later.

"Dad thinks we're crazy," she said.

"What did you tell him?"

"The truth, sort of. We're going to check out some places for your Heritage Fair project. Do you have the key?"

Gwyn patted his pocket.

When they stepped outside, the wind was rising with a hollow moan. "Oh, great," Maddie said. "Just what we need." Power lines and branches shook, their ice casings shattering all around.

Gwyn grinned. "Frozen fireworks."

"I'm glad somebody appreciates this weather."

The streets were empty, but Gwyn could hear the scrape and rumble of snowploughs nearby, cut now and then by the high-pitched bleating of backup alarms. The city must have thought the storm was ending. The crust on the snow was fragile as old bones, shattering with every step. In spite of his bravado about dead things, Gwyn wondered what they were getting into. To distract himself, he started talking about what he'd discovered the night before.

"Turns out there are lots of pterosaurs in the Solnhofen Limestone. They still find them. People used to think they used their wings to swim, like penguins, and after they knew about evolution, they thought pterosaurs must be some kind of link between bats and birds."

"But they're not, right? So what are they, a distinct species?"

"A whole bunch of species — over a hundred that we know of. Some were the size of chickens, some as big as small airplanes." Maddie smiled as if he were stretching the truth, so Gwyn rushed on. "No, really. The biggest ones had twelve-metre wingspans. We don't even know how many species there were. It looks like a lot are missing from the fossils we have now."

"But they were a kind of dinosaur, and birds evolved from dinosaurs, so aren't they related to birds?"

"They're related to birds like we're related to kangaroos. No, more distant than that. Pterosaurs split off from dinosaurs really early. They're pretty sure *Tyrannosaurus rex* is part of the line that birds evolved from, so T. Rex was closer to a chicken than the pterosaurs were."

"What happened to them?"

Gwyn shrugged. "We don't know. Not yet."

"You're funny. You think we'll find out?"

"I do. Look at Dad's work. Genetics can tell us stuff people never imagined we'd know."

"Even about failed animals like pterosaurs?"

"Hey, don't say 'failed'! They lived for about one hundred and sixty million years. Can you imagine? Our ancestor species only split off from the apes about two million years ago. Think about it, Maddie. Once, the skies were full of them, just like birds today. That was over sixty million years ago."

"I don't know, Gwyn. When you and Dad talk like that, my mind boggles." Gwyn had to laugh, but she went on. "No, really. I can almost hear it go *boing*. I can't get my mind around millions of years." She shook her head. "Let's cut across by The Rooms to keep away from the ice bombs."

They passed The Rooms and the police station, coming out on Harvey Road by a granite monument. Gwyn vaguely remembered it was for some people who had died when a dance hall burned down during World War II. The Knights of Columbus something or other. They had overshot the Kirk by quite a bit. There was a steep drop, a cliff really, on the other side of the road, with a chain-link fence running along the sidewalk to keep people from falling off. They crossed and looked into a parking lot below, mostly empty today. It was a long way down.

Gwyn remembered something. "Dad went to school here, didn't he?"

"Holloway School. Yes. They tore it down before we were born."

Gwyn stepped forward and kicked the chain-link fence hard. Ice rattled off, falling into the pit below with a sound like breaking dishes. "Why did they do that? They're always tearing things down."

Maddie didn't try to answer, pointing away from the Kirk. "Come on, the stairs are this way."

Gwyn looked back in the opposite direction, where a wooden passageway led into the second storey of the church. "What about that door? It leads into the building. Maybe we should look there first."

"Right, I bet it's been used every Sunday since it was built, which was probably after Daniel died, but I'm sure we'll find it totally undisturbed with an antique lock on the door."

Gwyn grinned. Sometimes, she sounded just like their father. "After you, Sherlock."

A lane with steep steps led down to the street below, but snow had smoothed it into an unbroken slope. They had to cling to the fence beside the lane to keep from slipping, and Gwyn couldn't look around until they reached the bottom. Harvey Road was out of sight here, the back side of The Rooms looming above. They were only a few blocks from home, but the streets were totally unfamiliar. Long's Hill ran at an angle in front of them, bridging the incline between the road above and downtown below. Old houses lined the opposite side, most of them plain wooden boxes. On this side of the street, the parking lot stretched from where they stood to the grounds of the Kirk, backed by the raw rock cliff they had looked down from moments before. Even with a covering of snow, the place was desolate as an empty socket.

"It must have looked better when the other buildings were here," Gwyn said.

"It did," Maddie said. "Gran showed me a photograph once. There were two big brick buildings, side by side, Dad's school and another. One of them even had a bell tower."

"Why did they leave it like this? It's hideous."

"I don't know." Maddie sounded annoyed, but not at Gwyn. "It's depressing here. Let's get this over with."

She was sure they weren't going to find anything. Gwyn could hear it in her voice. There was no reason to think otherwise, but Gwyn's stomach began to flip-flop as they crossed the parking lot. The Kirk was set on a small rise of its own, so they had to struggle up another set of snow-smoothed stairs, these ones wooden. As they did, the key in Gwyn's pocket seemed to sing with a whine he could almost hear, like a high-voltage hum in ice-coated cables. It had to be his imagination. There was an arched wooden door right in front of them, but it had a shiny new lock.

Maddie looked around. "It's not very big, is it? Let's walk around."

The front doors were not a place where anything could be hidden, and the other side of the church didn't seem to have any doors at all. "Looks like we can't walk around," Gwyn said. They retraced their steps. Near the rock wall on this side of the Kirk they found another arched wooden door with black iron fittings. "Look at that keyhole," Gwyn said, his voice rising. "This must be it."

"Unless the room is somewhere inside."

Gwyn shook his head. "This building is so small, all the space inside must be used." He slipped off his mitten and pulled the key from his pocket. It was uncomfortable to hold now, the current was so strong, but it fit perfectly and turned with a weighted click, as if the lock had been used yesterday. Gwyn and Maddie exchanged a look, then pressed on.

The door opened inward with a creak as a slash of grey winter storm light angled across a rough wooden floor to reveal bare brick walls.

"It looks like a closet," Maddie said.

Gwyn stepped inside. "I wish I'd thought to bring one of those flashlights."

"Wait a minute, let me in." Maddie pulled her house keys from her pocket, forcing Gwyn farther into the room. "I've never had to use this." She squeezed the end of her key chain and a beam of white LED light shot across the wall, bright but narrow, so it only illuminated a small spot. "Well, it's better than nothing. What do you see?"

"Not much. I think this place is empty." The depth of Gwyn's disappointment surprised him.

"Hamish? Is that you, laddie?" The voice floated out from the gloom, mild and civil, softly accented.

Gwyn grinned at Maddie, wondering how she'd played this trick, but even in the dim light, he could see she'd gone dead pale.

"Gwyn, that was mean. How did you do it?"

He was about to shake his head when the voice spoke again.

"It's awfully cold with that door open. Close it and I'll make a proper light so we can see."

Stupidly, they obeyed. A ghost, Gwyn thought. It's Daniel's ghost. He ran through what he knew from ghost stories and scary movies. Someone whose life was interrupted would find it hard to let go, and this had been Daniel's church. Why not here? Gwyn's heart pounded painfully, but there was nothing scary or evil in the voice, only a reassuring uncertainty.

"Who are you?" Maddie said, her voice shaking. Without waiting, she shone a beam of light around the room. It caught something.

"A model pterosaur!" The thought of ghosts went right out of Gwyn's head. Daniel must have left the model here. It was small, about the size of a chicken, with high wing bones folded back over its body and a beak like a parrot's. It stood on four feet, the front ones attached to the wings, the hind ones skinny and bowed. It had a long neck and bright, round eyes.

It blinked.

"Gwyn. It blinked."

But Gwyn had already made up his mind. "Don't be silly. How could it blink? It's just your light."

"That lamp is awfully bright, miss. Turn it down, please, if you dinna mind?"

Maddie grabbed Gwyn's shoulder as her keys fell. The place should have gone dark, but a soft, green light filled the room before they could move. The pterosaur was glowing.

"Bioluminescence," Gwyn said, almost reverently.

"Gwyn, that's no model." Maddie sounded sick.

"Did you think I was some stuffed beastie?" The pterosaur sounded amused. "Hamish, Daniel must have told you about me by now." The accent was soft but pronounced. "You" sounded like "*ye*" and "about" like "*aboot*." The pterosaur wasn't big enough to be frightening. Intelligence shone from his eyes, and the beak made him look as if he was smiling. Gwyn's fear vanished.

"Hamish was my great-grandfather." He said this as gently as he could.

The pterosaur blinked. "I've slept an awfully long time, have I? Well, it wouldn'a be the first time." When he spoke again, his voice was soft with sadness. "And Daniel must be long gone. I shall miss him. He was a dragon keeper the likes of which I hadn'a seen in centuries."

"Dragon keeper?" Gwyn asked.

"Aye, laddie. What do you think you're looking at?"

"A pterosaur. You're a pterosaur."

"*Tero-soar*? I dinna ken what that might be. *I* am a dragon." He sounded annoyed.

"Oh my gosh," Maddie said. "You're the Rae dragon, aren't you?"

A crest rose on the pterosaur's head. "Aye, that I am."

"Don't be ridiculous, look at him. He's a pterosaur. We've found the only living one on the planet." This was an incredible find. They'd be famous.

"I gi' you that, laddie. I am the last of my kind. I have been now for over a thousand years."

"And it's our job to look after you, isn't it?" Maddie's voice was filled with wonder.

"You're a clever lass. What's your name?"

"Maddie," she said as she retrieved her keys from the floor.

The dragon made a noise with his beak that sounded like stones grinding together. "Aye, it would be. I'm pleased to make your acquaintance, Miss Maddie Rae." He sounded very much like a Victorian gentleman, and he was genuinely delighted.

"And this is my brother, Gwyn. What are you called?"

The dragon said something totally unpronounceable that began with a C and seemed to contain a lot of *augh*s. "But nobody speaks that language now. It means Hermit Crab, so generally, I'm called Hermit."

"'H,'" Maddie cried, triumphant. "You're the 'H' in Daniel's notebooks. It all makes sense."

The conversation was getting away from Gwyn. Never mind if this pterosaur wanted to call itself a dragon, the animal was an important scientific discovery, not some kind of throwback to the Middle Ages. He was also miffed to find this thing so utterly charmed by Maddie.

"Now that you've woken me up, I'll be needing food and water quickly. Take me home, please," Hermit said.

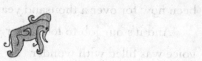

CHAPTER NINE

A DRAGON IN THE HOUSE

"I sn't this your home?" Maddie asked.

"You're joking. I live wherever you live. Daniel only put me here while he was gone away." It sounded like "*gang awa*" so it took Gwyn a moment to understand. Then, Hermit added, "Something terrible happened, I take it? Daniel would never have abandoned me."

"There was a shipwreck," Maddie said. "He never reached Boston."

The dragon's crest fell and his beak touched the floor. "Poor Daniel. He was heartbroken when James died and then he died too. So Hamish never even knew I existed. That was one reason Daniel wanted to bring him here, so he could become the next dragon keeper. Well, at least he got to live a normal life. Being a dragon keeper's no an easy task. But I really must eat soon. Can we go, please?"

"Of course," Maddie said. She seemed to take it for granted that the pterosaur would come home with them.

Gwyn hesitated. If Hermit admitted that looking after him was not easy, just how hard would it be? How could they even take him outside? Gwyn was suddenly grateful for the blizzard, but people could still look out their windows. "Maddie, what if anyone sees us?"

Hermit made that grinding sound again and Gwyn realized it was his way of laughing. "Do you think anyone else can see me, laddie? Only the children of Madoca can perceive the dragon. To everyone else, I'm invisible."

Madonna? Who was she? Gwyn wished Hermit wouldn't refer to himself as "the dragon." It was too bizarre.

Maddie seemed more comfortable. "So it *is* genetic! That's why no one else could read the parts of Daniel's notebooks that were about you. What about the key?"

"Just take me outside if you want to understand about the key. I'll be weak for the first few days. I'm afraid you'll have to carry me."

Maddie knelt as if this were the most ordinary request in the world. Gwyn always knew she was brave, but really. Pterosaur or dragon, taking this little guy home was a big step.

Hermit scrambled up her knee and onto her shoulders, where he curled around her neck like some kind of exotic stole. "Ready," he said. "This jacket is lovely. I've got a good grip."

"You're so light!" Maddie said as she stood.

"Any flying creature is bound to be," Gwyn reminded her. He would have been afraid to let the dragon get up on him like that, but seeing Hermit on Maddie's shoulders, he felt a stab of jealousy. He'd always imagined the dragon would be his pet.

"You'll need to hang on," Maddie said. "The weather's terrible."

"Aye," the dragon said. "Daniel could never get over the weather here. Much worse than Scotland."

"But why did he come here?" Gwyn asked. "I've always wondered."

The dragon said a word that sounded like someone clearing their throat. "Och, that's a story for another day. We must hurry. I have to eat and drink directly when I've been asleep for so long."

Gwyn nodded. "You'll get dehydrated if your metabolism kicks in while you're running on empty."

Hermit stared at him. "I have no clue what you said just then, laddie."

Maddie laughed. "It's going to take time before we understand one another. Let's get you home."

Outside, back in the storm, Gwyn was almost surprised to find everything unchanged.

"Now then, close the door and watch what happens,"
Hermit commanded. For someone so small, he certainly
was bossy.

Gwyn pushed the door shut and they waited. For
a long moment, nothing happened. Just when he was
sure the little guy was playing a joke on them, the out-
line of the door began to blur and fade. In seconds, it
was gone, revealing a blank brick wall.

"There never was a room, was there?" Maddie asked
as they started to walk away. She seemed oddly comfortable with all of this.

"Well, there was and there wasn'a," Hermit replied.
"It isn'a easy to explain—MERCIFUL HEAVENS! Has
there been a war?" He was staring at the parking lot.

"Two wars, but that's not what happened here," Maddie replied. "Um, Hermit, could you loosen your grip a
bit?"

"Oh, pardon me. What did happen?"

Gwyn sighed. "Progress, I think."

"Come on," Maddie said. "We need to get home."

On the street beside the parking lot, ice bombs
exploded again as the power lines swayed in the wind.
"The telegraph must be awfully popular these days," Hermit said, looking up.

Gwyn shook his head. "Boy, do you have a lot of catching up to do."

The trip home was all uphill, and Gwyn and Maddie panted as they rushed through the ice-crusted snow. Gwyn tried to make sense of it. Hermit said he was over a thousand years old, so he must exist outside the laws of nature, yet he needed food and water. It would take time to understand. What did dragons eat, anyway? Tender young maidens. Gwyn began to smile, then he looked at Maddie with Hermit wrapped around her neck, and suddenly it was a very bad joke. What if—no, that was crazy. Daniel would never have devoted himself to a creature who feasted on the flesh of young girls. That was something out of a horror movie. Hermit didn't seem aggressive. Don't think dragon, he ordered himself. Okay, what would a pterosaur eat? Probably live things. Gwyn had known a few kids who kept snakes. The idea of trapping or buying live prey for Hermit was repulsive. Well, there was only one way to find out.

"What do you eat, Hermit?"

"What month is this?"

"February."

"Oh, that's a shame. Mostly turnip and carrots, then. I eat fish and shellfish too, but the older I get, the more I prefer vegetables. Spinach is my favourite, but you'll no find any this time of year, of course."

Gwyn gave a giant sigh of relief.

"We should be able to find some spinach," Maddie said. "Things really have changed."

"But Maddie, where are we going to keep him?" Gwyn asked.

"I sleep in the same room as you," Hermit said, in a way that left no room for argument. "You may take turns if you wish. James and Daniel took turns, month about."

"So James knew about you too?" Maddie asked.

"Of course. And their father before them, and before that, their grandmother. She would be your great-great-great-great-grandmother, Jane Ballentyne. She was a bonnie lass."

"Wow, it's too bad our grandmother didn't meet you. She took a real interest in our family history after Grandpa died."

"And Hamish was his father? Well, she wouldn'a have been able to see me, laddie, but I could have told him stories. And you must be the children of his son since you have the Rae name. Your father will be able to see me too. You'll have to introduce us."

Gwyn and Maddie stopped walking.

"What's wrong?" Hermit asked. "Your father will want to meet me, of course."

"Our father's a scientist. He studies genetics," Gwyn replied.

"I've never seen a genetic," Hermit said. "Is it anything like a caribou?"

"Oh dear," Maddie said.

Gwyn could see she was trying not to laugh, but it wasn't entirely funny. "My father doesn't need to know about you right away," he said quickly. "That would only confuse things."

Maddie rolled her eyes at the understatement. If their father reacted as the scientist he was, Hermit might be whisked off to some lab for study. Gwyn knew he couldn't let that happen. His connection to this creature—pterosaur or dragon—was immediate and powerful. He looked at Maddie, her eyes shining as she carried Hermit, and he knew she felt the same.

They walked on in silence until Hermit lifted his head as if he were sniffing the air. "There's something wrong," he said. "Everything's so different."

Maddie nodded. "It is, but we'll help you get used to the changes."

"No, it's more than that. It's as if—" Gwyn could see him straining to find the words. "—as if the whole world were badly out of tune. Things spinning out of control . . ." His voice trailed off. His eyes looked out of focus.

"We have to get you inside fast," Gwyn said as they turned onto their street. "You need food and warmth. Don't worry, we're almost home."

"If Dad's still in his study, we can go in the front and get Hermit upstairs without being seen," Maddie said.

Gwyn nodded. The stairs were just inside the front door. "I'll go first. Wait here. If I see Dad, I'll grab the snow shovel and come out again."

Gwyn slipped inside. "We're home," he called to the back of the house.

A muffled "That's nice" told him his father was still hard at work. He unlaced his boots, opened the door and waved Maddie in, reaching to lift Hermit from her shoulders.

But the creature pulled back. "Never touch my wing bones!"

"Did you say something?" Tom called from his study.

"Just talking," Maddie replied.

"Put your hands under my front legs," Hermit whispered. Gwyn did, lifting him by the armpits, or maybe wingpits. The little guy was incredibly light, his small body soft. His wing bones stuck up, level with his head, which was huge compared to the rest of him. Hermit wrapped his long neck around Gwyn's shoulder, his beak resting on the arm of his jacket. Earlier, Gwyn had been afraid to hold Hermit, but the little pterosaur felt good, oddly enough, as if he belonged there. He was shivering, though.

"Get something to eat," Gwyn whispered to Maddie. "And maybe a hot drink."

On the second-floor landing, Gwyn hesitated. Should he go into the bathroom for water? Downstairs, he could hear Maddie talking. Their father must have come out of his study. Gwyn scooted up to his own room on the third floor.

"This room is a mess!" Hermit said.

"I wasn't expecting company," Gwyn grumbled.

"Never mind, then, laddie. I'm sure you can do better. I had Daniel and James keeping their rooms tidy well before your age."

Gwyn had always pictured the dragon as some kind of super-pet. Now he wondered if Hermit was going to be worse than an extra mother. He swiped a pile of junk off the surface of his dresser, books, magazines and batteries spilling to the floor, and opened a drawer, piling warm clothes on top. "Climb down. We have to get you warmed up."

Hermit settled into the jumble of clothes, but he was still shivering. Not good enough, Gwyn thought. He pulled the duvet from the floor, spreading it neatly over the sheets and blankets rumpled at the bottom of his bed. "Come on, let me move you." When Hermit was settled, Gwyn banked the sweaters and fleeces from his dresser around him for warmth.

"After so long on a cold floor, this is lovely." Hermit rested his chin on the duvet, his body compact like a cat's with his wing bones folded back. He closed his eyes and his breathing slowed.

Gwyn sat by his pillow, watching. By the time Maddie arrived with a tray, the shivering had stopped. "I think he's asleep," he whispered as Maddie set the tray down on his dresser.

She frowned. "He shouldn't sleep until he's eaten." She pointed to a steaming cup. "I found an old package of soup-in-a-cup from last summer. Tomato basil."

"That was lucky," Gwyn said. Their mother only bought processed foods for camping. Avoiding his wing bones, Gwyn gave Hermit a nudge in the ribs. "Hermit, wake up."

"Hermit," Maddie called. He opened his eyes at the sound of her voice. "Sit up and drink some soup," she commanded.

"Too hot," he said before the cup even touched his beak.

"I'll put it on the windowsill. It will cool quickly there." Hermit's eyes closed again. He swayed.

"Look, lettuce and cucumber."

Hermit's eyes sprang open. "That's a treat. Where do you find them this time of the year?"

"At the supermarket," Maddie replied.

"Your market must be super indeed." The dragon's beak was amazingly agile. The salad disappeared like magic.

"Good. Now, try the soup," Maddie coaxed.

"Blech!" Hermit said when he tasted it. "This is awful. Too salty."

Maddie grinned. "Our mother would love you. What do you usually drink?"

"India tea, black with sugar. Two spoonfuls if you can spare it."

"Tea?"

"Aye, I love a good cup of tea. Of course, before they had tea I drank water."

"Before they had tea? When was that?" Gwyn asked.

"Tea arrived in the 1600s," Hermit said. "That was an interesting century. Isaac Newton, gravity and all."

"Hermit, you're not really that old, are you?" Maddie asked.

"I dinna expect you to believe everything right away," Hermit replied. "It's always a shock to the new dragon keepers when I've been gone a long time."

"It's happened before?"

"Oh, aye. I slept right through the last half of the 1300s, well into the middle of the 1400s, because of the Black Death. Just as well. Daniel and James reviewed it with me when they were boys so I could see what I'd missed. It was a turbulent period in Scottish history, even without all they people dying of the plague."

"But how have you lived so long? Why?" Gwyn asked.

Hermit sank down onto the bed. "Not now, laddie. I'm fair exhausted."

"Wait, Hermit. Drink some water before you sleep." Maddie disappeared down the stairs, returning with water. Hermit dipped his beak in. It was grey like the rest of him, but translucent. Though Gwyn could see the dragon's tongue working while he sipped the water, the beak looked strong enough to puncture a can.

Maddie looked around. "I don't think he should sleep on the bed," she said as Hermit finished his drink. "What if you hit his wing bones in your sleep? What if Dad were to come in? He needs a place of his own."

"A lair," Hermit agreed, his voice fading.

"How about the top of the wardrobe?" Maddie asked. There were no closets in the house, so every bedroom had a wooden wardrobe, and there was room between the top of Gwyn's and the sloping attic ceiling. Maddie climbed onto the dresser to look into it. "It's a nice space. The moulding sticks up above the top of the wardrobe like a railing. When he gets in there, you won't see him at all. But it's really dusty. I'll have to vacuum." She shook her head when she climbed down. "Dad thought salad and instant soup was a strange snack. He's going to wonder if I get the vacuum cleaner."

Gwyn looked at the cactus on his windowsill. "Tell him I knocked my plant over."

Maddie's forehead wrinkled. "I don't like to lie."

That was an understatement. It was one of the things Gwyn liked about Maddie. Ask her a question and she'd tell the truth, even if she'd rather not. He walked over to his windowsill and cuffed the cactus. It fell to the floor, dirt spilling out of the plastic pot. "Oh look, I knocked my plant over."

Maddie smiled. "I'll get the vacuum."

As she was leaving, Gwyn had another thought. "Maddie, what about—you know, potty?"

"Old newspapers," Hermit croaked.

Maddie nodded. "I'll get some from recycling."

When she left, Gwyn looked at Hermit, stretched out on his duvet among the fleeces and sweaters. He looked so warm and relaxed, Gwyn could have sworn the little guy was smiling.

CHAPTER TEN

MADDIE BECOMES A VEGETARIAN

At supper that night, Maddie made an announcement. "I've decided to stop eating meat for a while." Gwyn noticed she did not say she wanted to become a vegetarian.

Everyone stared. Tom shook his head. "Maddie, you're the original carnivore. Do you know what your first solid food was?"

Maddie nodded. "Roast lamb." Their father told the story from time to time. Gwyn could see it didn't make her happy to remember it now.

Tom smiled. "I couldn't keep up with you. I was trying to carve a leg of lamb and every time I looked at your high chair, the bowl was empty."

Annette's forehead creased. "I knew this might happen. It's something teenage girls do. So, what kind? Vegan? Lacto-ovo?"

Maddie frowned. "I don't know what you mean."

"Vegans don't eat any animal products, not even cheese or eggs. Is that what you want?"

"No!" Maddie cried.

"Okay, so you'll eat dairy and eggs. That's good. Otherwise, I'd be worried about your calcium and zinc. What about fish? Some people eat fish, too."

"Sure," Maddie said. "I like fish."

She likes beef and pork and chicken and lamb, too, Gwyn thought. And moose. Maddie loved moose meat. She was doing this for Hermit.

"Great," Annette said. "It will do us all good to cut back on meat."

Gwyn groaned inwardly. Maddie could at least have warned him.

"How's the Heritage Fair project coming?" Tom asked. "Find anything interesting today?"

Gwyn avoided Maddie's eyes. "We just went to look at the Kirk. It was smaller than I'd expected. I've got my topic now," he continued, steering the conversation to safer ground. "Daniel made a study of flight and flighted animals." He looked down at his plate, at the lovely chicken breast that was about to become extinct at this table, attacking it while he asked the next question. "Dad, are there any books on pterosaurs in the university library?"

"Probably. We can check the online catalogue after supper."

"Did people know about pterosaurs in Daniel's time?" Annette asked.

"Yes," Gwyn and his father replied together, and everyone laughed.

"I found a clipping in Daniel's notebook," Gwyn explained. "From *The Times* of London, about the discovery of a fossil in this place in Germany."

Tom nodded. "They were identified as distinct creatures almost a century before people began to think in terms of evolution."

"Well, I'm glad you've got your topic, Gwyn," Annette said. "Speaking of school, Maddie, I was talking to Sunny today and she's been in touch with your teacher. It sounds like you're all going to learn to do that tablet weaving."

"Thanks for reminding me. Ms. Keats wants us to bring in old cereal boxes. She's been reading up, and we can make weaving tablets out of them."

"Have a look in the recycling bags. I'm sure you'll find some."

"See? It's a good thing I didn't take the recycling in last weekend when you asked me," Tom joked.

"I'm looking forward to learning. Ms. Keats said she'd never heard of it before, but here's something funny — there's a boy in my class who already knows how to do it."

"I'll have to tell Sunny. She'll be surprised. How did he learn?" Annette asked.

"He used to live near a place like L'Anse aux Meadows in Norway, where people dressed in Viking costumes and taught visitors crafts. Ms. Keats got really excited when he told us."

"How did he end up here?" Gwyn asked. Newfoundland didn't attract many immigrants.

"His father works in the offshore."

"Oh, that makes sense," Tom said. "The offshore oil industry brings people from Norway. They fit in well here."

Maddie shook her head. "Jonas isn't fitting in. He knits, he weaves, he even sewed himself a shirt. He was really proud of it until . . ." she trailed off.

"Are the other kids giving him a hard time?" Annette asked.

"They sure are. 'Jonas, fashion queen,' they're calling him."

Gwyn's mother turned bright red. "What's wrong with teenagers? Why do they think everyone has to be exactly alike?"

Gwyn stared at her. He'd assumed there was something wrong with him for feeling that way.

"You remember how it was," Tom replied. "Everyone frantic to fit in."

"I wasn't like that, and neither were you, from what you've told me." A smile softened her face. "With your bug collection and your telescope." She turned to Maddie. "Why don't you invite this boy for supper sometime? We could make him feel more at home."

Maddie blushed bright pink. "Oh, I couldn't. He might get the wrong idea. You know." She looked miserable. "I'm really not ready for dating and stuff."

"Hard life, being a teenager," Tom joked, but there was real sympathy in his voice. Maddie nodded.

"Well, if you change your mind, he's welcome. We wouldn't treat him like a boyfriend or anything, Maddie," Annette said. "Dessert anyone?"

With a shiver, Gwyn remembered there was a real live pterosaur sleeping on top of his wardrobe. It was like something out of a dream. "I think I'll skip dessert tonight."

Annette stared at him. "I thought I was kidding. Are you feeling okay?"

"Fine," Gwyn said. "I'd just like to see if we can find any books about pterosaurs." Too late, Gwyn wondered if his father would want to use the computer in his bedroom.

But Tom said, "Come into my study and we'll check out the university library."

As they left, Gwyn heard Maddie say, "I think I'll make a little salad to take upstairs." She did not say *she* wanted a salad, or that *she* was going to eat it.

Gwyn and his father found a handful of titles in the university library catalogue on pterosaurs, and Tom printed off the list. "This is great," Gwyn said. "I'll pick a few for my project."

Back upstairs, Gwyn found Maddie in his bedroom with an empty salad bowl. "He's already gone back to sleep," she whispered. "He's still shaky."

"Do you think he's okay? What if he's sick?" Gwyn had a vision of trying to talk to a vet about his invisible pet dragon.

"He said he'll be fine in a few days. We just have to take his word for it. He used the papers before he went back to sleep, so his digestive tract is working." She pointed to the corner where they'd left old newspapers. Gwyn was almost afraid to look, but he found something like bird droppings—odourless, inoffensive, hardly more than a stain.

"You found some books?" Maddie asked, noticing the list Gwyn was carrying. "Is there one on 'care and feeding'?"

"I wish." Gwyn glanced to the top of the wardrobe where the tip of Hermit's tail draped over the wooden moulding. "So some pterosaurs survived when the rest became extinct sixty million years ago. Think about it.

Sixty million years is a long time. If pterosaurs were warm-blooded like dinosaurs, and intelligent like songbirds or parrots, you could end up with something as smart as Hermit. Couldn't you?"

"So what is this? Science or magic? I'm completely confused." Maddie rubbed her forehead.

"Well, it has to be a bit of both, doesn't it? If Hermit's been around for over a thousand years, that's not science. Nothing could possibly live that long." Gwyn looked up at the wardrobe again. Hermit's tail had disappeared. "When he's awake again, we'll ask him about it."

"Does this mean all those stories about dragons are real?" Maddie went to Gwyn's computer, opened the search engine and typed "dragon." She got millions of hits. Gwyn stood behind her and they began to read, skipping past the brand name and fantasy game articles. When they finally finished skimming through, it was almost bedtime.

"So," Maddie said, "in China, dragons are good, but in Europe, they're bad."

" . . . except in Wales, where the red dragon represents the people in Britain before the Anglo Saxons came. Anglo Saxons were sort of like Vikings, weren't they?"

"Very good, laddie." Hermit was peering down from the top of his lair. "By the time I was born, there was only a small group of dragons left in Orkney, and a few in the

Norselands that the Vikings hadn'a yet killed. But I have always wondered about Wales."

"How did you know they were the only dragons left?" Gwyn asked.

"We could call to one another over hundreds of miles."

"Infrasound, I bet, just like elephants," Gwyn cried.

"Go on, Hermit," Maddie urged. "What about Wales?"

"Stories have been told about the red dragon of Wales for centuries, and the people of Wales are the original inhabitants of Britain, just as the people in my home were on the Orkney Isles. I've always wondered if they might have loved and revered the dragons, just as your ancestors did."

"So one of our ancestors saved you?" Maddie asked.

"Aye, Madoca. A powerful magician and a great friend to the dragons. Her people knew there was nothing evil about us. We kept their knowledge for them before they knew how to write."

Maddie pointed to the computer. "But so much is written about evil, fire-breathing dragons. How did that happen?"

Hermit yawned. "Viking nonsense. It's a long story and we'll have plenty of time to talk. I still need to rest. Could I have a wee sip of water before I go back to sleep?"

"I'll get some. Gwyn, we should keep a water bowl in here from now on."

Gwyn wanted to know everything, but Hermit could hardly keep his eyes open and it would have been cruel to badger him with questions. Later, though, when he lay in the dark, Gwyn couldn't sleep. It was hard to believe any of this was real. How are we going to keep such a big secret from Mom and Dad? he wondered. The idea made him queasy. But it was exciting, too. Hermit was like a pet, only better. Gwyn wondered if he could sneak his dragon into school one day, just for fun.

Gwyn finally drifted into a light sleep and Hermit was with him at school, curled around his shoulders, but everyone could see him. "What is that, Rae? The new fashion statement? What are you, a fashion queen?" Strange boys sneered at Gwyn.

"This is my dragon," he shouted back. "I'm the only one who has one." This didn't impress them.

"Ohhh, a dragon. I'm so scared."

"Come on, dragon, breathe fire on me. Scratch my eyes out."

"Here comes a sword."

They started jabbing Hermit with their pens. The little dragon's terror shot through Gwyn's bloodstream. A pen stabbed Gwyn's chest and he woke, his heart pounding in his ears. It was morning.

Never, he told himself as he got up. I will never take Hermit to school. When he looked at the papers in the

corner of his room, they were completely clean with only
a faint crinkle to show Hermit had used them. The dragon
did not wake while Gwyn got ready for school, not even
when he softly called Hermit's name a few times.

CHAPTER ELEVEN

Λτ Home with Dragon

On the short walk to their schools, Gwyn and Maddie agreed to meet at home for lunch, though their lunch periods overlapped only by fifteen minutes. "It's better that way, really," Maddie said when she left Gwyn in front of her school. "Hermit will have more time with us."

"If he's awake."

The memory of his dream nagged at Gwyn, but he said nothing about it. He found it impossible to concentrate in school, though. Worry wrapped around his neck like something with claws.

When Gwyn came home at lunchtime, Hermit was sitting on the kitchen counter, listening to music. It seemed reckless to have him down here. "What if Dad comes home?" he asked Maddie.

She pointed to the schedule on the fridge. "He's in the middle of a class. Hermit didn't know music could be recorded."

The little dragon looked better, his saucer eyes bright and alert. "I canna believe it," he cried. "Music whenever you want! We had to hire musicians or go to concerts. This would have made Daniel so happy. He loved Mendelssohn, and after he came here, he never heard that music again."

"I think Mom might have some Mendelssohn," Maddie replied. "I'll check." She came back from the living room with a CD. "The He-brides Overture and *Midsummer Night's Dream*."

"*Heb-ri-des*," Hermit corrected. "Three syllables. Also a group of islands off the coast of Scotland, like Orkney where I was born. Could we hear that, please?"

Gwyn sat down to eat, but he couldn't take his eyes off Hermit as Maddie put the CD on. It was fancy orchestra music, nothing Gwyn would ever have listened to alone. Hermit swayed his tail in time to it as if he were conducting. How could anyone think these creatures were evil?

"So tell us, Hermit," Gwyn said, "how did dragons get such a bad reputation?"

Hermit's tail stopped swaying. "Let's say the Vikings got the upper hand, and the people who cared for the dragons, well, they disappeared."

Gwyn shook his head. "You said we descended from them. If they'd disappeared, we wouldn't be here."

"I dinna mean the actual people. I mean their culture, their identity."

"Who were they?" Maddie asked.

Hermit said another of those unpronounceable words. "That's what they called themselves, but no one knows that now. People call them by the name the Romans gave them—the Picts."

"The Romans? You mean like the Roman Empire? Didn't they live in Rome? You're talking about Scotland."

Hermit shook his head. "Do they teach you nothing in school these days? The Roman Empire covered most of southern Europe and a good part of the east. They came to Britain but they could never defeat your ancestors. The Romans called them the Picts, *di Picti*. It might mean 'painted people' or 'people who make drawings.'"

"You don't know?" Maddie asked.

Hermit snorted. "I never met a Roman. That was long before my time."

"So these people, the Picts, you say they disappeared. How?" she asked.

"An evil Viking seer put a curse on them. Then, over the first century of my life, the Picts just disappeared as a people, through wars and political alliances. They vanished."

"But they didn't really disappear. We must know something about them."

Hermit shook his head. "No one knows about their gods or their stories now. No one knows how important the dragons were to them, or that there were dragons. Even the language they spoke is forgotten. I'm the last person who speaks it."

Gwyn almost smiled when Hermit called himself a person, but he stopped himself. Hermit was more of a person than some of the goons at his school.

"But you know so much about them," Maddie said. "Can't you find a way to tell people?"

Hermit shook his head. "Daniel's father, Alexander, thought the same thing. I told him everything I knew about my people and he wrote it all down. He left the dragons out. We argued about that but in the end I understood why. He printed a pamphlet, 'The Truth About the Picts,' it was called. He was sure it was going to change everything."

"What happened?"

"People just laughed. Fanciful nonsense, they called it," he lifted his chin, "even though we'd left out the dragons, the most important part, because Alex said people wouldn'a believe it. The learned gentlemen of the day said Alex couldn'a possibly have known these things, that he was just making them up. Alex was a young lad, in his early twenties, and he was sensitive by nature. It nearly crushed him. Later, he wouldn'a let James or Daniel try anything like that. But Daniel kept a copy of the pamphlet."

"I wonder if it's with Daniel's papers in the archives," Maddie said. "I told Hermit about the papers and your project while we were having lunch," she told Gwyn.

The crest on Hermit's head went up. "I'm very pleased, laddie, to know you're interested in your family history. I'll be delighted to help you."

"I think we should go to the Mews Annex after school today as usual," Maddie added.

Gwyn put his sandwich down. "You've got to be kidding."

"No. You have to keep working on your project, and Hermit says he still needs extra sleep. Finish up with Daniel's papers this week and then you can start to work at home."

"It will be at least a week before I'm back to my old self," Hermit said. "I'm already starting to fade." He yawned. "See?"

Gwyn thought Hermit might be pretending to be exhausted just to get him to concentrate on his project, but there was no point in arguing. He put the wrappings from his sandwich into his backpack, hiding the evidence that they'd been home for lunch. Maddie had already washed Hermit's dishes and carefully replaced them in the cupboard, not trusting them to the dishwasher.

"Time to go," she said. "I'll see you after school."

Hermit rested his head on the counter, his eyes drifting shut.

"Come on," Gwyn said. "It looks like you're ready for bed."

"Maddie put an extra blanket on your bed for me," Hermit murmured as Gwyn carried him upstairs.

Gwyn found a clean fleece throw on his bed.

"I've never seen such a soft blanket. What do you call it?" Hermit asked.

"It's a fleece."

"A fleece, you say? You must have wonderful new varieties of sheep."

Gwyn didn't try to explain as he pushed the blanket onto the top of the wardrobe.

"Maddie's a very thoughtful lassie," Hermit added as Gwyn boosted him up to his lair. "Oh, could you do something for me, Gwyn? Make your bed and tidy up a wee bit. When I wake, I find it painful to look down on such a mess."

Gwyn sighed. "Have a good sleep, Hermit."

He made the bed. It only took a minute and it seemed natural to do anything that made Hermit happy.

CHAPTER TWELVE

BEFRIENDING A VIKING

When Maddie met Gwyn outside her school at the end of the day, she was smiling. "We made weaving tablets in my textile arts class today. I'll show you tonight."

"You're really interested in this stuff, aren't you?"

Maddie nodded. "I am, but it's more than that. This class is a break from all the others. Nobody from the soccer team would go near this group. The kids scared me at first, some of them look so strange, with pierced eyebrows and stuff. There's a girl who changes her hair colour just about every week—purple, blue, pink, orange. But it's fun to see what she's done. Sometimes we clap when she comes in with a new colour, and not in a mean way. I expected these kids to be nasty or unfriendly because I'm not like them but they're very—I don't know—accepting. They just take you for what you are."

"I thought you said they were mean to that Norwegian kid."

"Not them. The ones who pick on Jonas aren't in that class, they're just the creeps who are mean to anyone." Maddie shook her head. "Let's not talk about them. What are you doing today?"

"I've got to get to the end of the 'D' notebook."

"Now we know what 'D' stands for," Maddie said.

"Dragon? I guess so. It's still a little hard to believe, isn't it?"

Maddie laughed. "It's not hard to believe, Gwyn, it's impossible."

At the Mews Annex, Maddie opened the finding aid that catalogued all of Daniel's papers.

"Look, Gwyn," she said after a moment, "Daniel gave a lecture on his ideas about flight."

"Good. Copy down the file number for me, will you?"

"Oh, here's something else," Maddie added. "A pamphlet written by Alexander McCall Rae. I think he was Daniel's father. Maybe I'll read that, too." She was doing a bad job of pretending she wasn't excited as she went to find Dr. Mews.

When he brought the box to Maddie's desk, Dr. Mews asked, "How's your project coming along?" Gwyn remembered how cranky he'd been when they'd first shown up. Somehow, he'd started to treat them like friends.

"We're just about finished here," Gwyn said. "This should be our last week."

"Really?" Dr. Mews sounded disappointed. He looked at Maddie. "How old are you?" he demanded.

"Fourteen?" Maddie sounded as if she were guessing.

"Oh, that's too bad. I could hire someone to work here in the summertime, a student. There are grants. They've been after me for years, but I never felt I could work with a young person. You'd suit me fine. Actually, either of you would, but you're both too young." He was turning away as Maddie caught his arm.

"Thank you very much, Dr. Mews. That's a real compliment."

Dr. Mews actually smiled.

You'd suit me fine. It wouldn't be a compliment, Gwyn thought, coming from anyone else, but Maddie was right.

She continued. "Maybe you'd like to see Gwyn's project when it's finished."

He shook his head. "I shouldn't. I've just been asked to help judge the provincial finals. If Gwyn's project is selected and I've already seen it, I would have to disqualify myself."

"You think Gwyn might make the provincial finals?" Maddie asked. Gwyn was already shaking his head.

"You never know. He's working with excellent source material. I'll let you get back to work."

Maddie opened the box, found the right file folder and lifted out a small, yellowed pamphlet. Gwyn itched to know what was in it, but he forced himself to concentrate on Daniel's notebook instead. He'd have more time to spend with Hermit when he finished here.

Knowing what they did now, Daniel's notebook made more sense. As he read the final pages, Gwyn could see that Daniel had been trying to figure out how Hermit's ancestors might have evolved. The evolution of dragons. How could Gwyn present *that* as his Heritage Fair project? Everyone would laugh at him, like they had laughed at Daniel's father. He glanced at Maddie. Her forehead had knotted as if she was having a hard time believing what she was reading. So had a lot of other people, from what Hermit had said. No, he'd need another angle. Maybe Hermit could help. Gwyn closed the book and shook his head. He was seriously thinking about asking a dragon for help. It was crazy. What was Hermit doing here? Why had he lived so long? They had to ask him soon.

"Finished?" Maddie asked.

"Yep. All done." Gwyn looked outside. The colour had bled from the sky, leaving it pale grey. Time to call it a day. His hand ached from taking notes and he could hardly wait to find out what Maddie had discovered. He shuffled through his papers and found the order form. "I'll give Dr. Mews this list of photos so he can get them printed for my project, then we can go."

They walked well away from the building before speaking. A February thaw had started, with puddles nestled on the ice like tiny, glacial lakes. The frozen snow from just a few days before was melting and the park looked like the end of an ice age.

"That's a sign of spring," Maddie said, nodding toward groups of kids who were hanging out in the bandshell. It was the first time they'd seen teenagers in the park.

"What was in that pamphlet?" Gwyn asked.

She shook her head. "No wonder people laughed at Alexander. All these stories about worshipping the sun and moon, about powerful magicians who were respected by everyone, even the chieftains. It would have been impossible to believe anyone could know that stuff."

"But he didn't write about the dragons?"

"No, he didn't, so I can see this big hole in the middle of what he's trying to describe that makes it even harder to understand."

"And we're related to these magicians?"

"That's what Hermit —"

Angry shouting interrupted Maddie and they turned to a group of boys clustered by the swings. One kid stood

alone in the middle. He was taller than any of them, but
Gwyn could see he was in trouble. The other boys took
turns shoving him.

"Faggot!" one of them yelled.

Gwyn's stomach lurched. It was just like his dream,
with everyone poking at Hermit.

Maddie took off. "Wait," Gwyn cried. "Maddie, stop!"
But she didn't listen. She ran straight into the middle of
the pack, where the tall boy stood, helpless.

"BACK OFF!" Maddie yelled. It was the same searing
anger she'd shown Tyler Cull. And even though Maddie and
the helpless boy were outnumbered three to one, the bullies
did exactly that, melting into the icy park without a word.

Gwyn's heart was pounding and he hadn't even
moved. How could Maddie do that? He wished he knew
the trick.

"Jonas," Maddie said, "are you okay?"

He nodded, though he was still pale. Gwyn remembered the name. This was the guy who sewed. He was
almost six feet tall but thin as a rail, so his height gave
him no advantage. His blond hair was straight and wispy.
He had a long, sharp nose and glasses with thick, square
frames. Maybe those glasses were fashionable in Norway,
but here, they were just plain odd. Gwyn could see why
he was in trouble. Even without the sewing, Jonas looked
like nobody else.

"Come on," Maddie said, "you're coming home with us."

Jonas looked dazed as he followed Maddie. Gwyn wondered if he had been scared witless, or if maybe it was just impossible to disobey Maddie when she was like this.

As they reached Gwyn, the boy spoke. His voice was soft and low and his English had a singsong, musical lilt. "This is something I wonder about English. Why do you call people 'gay' when everyone tries so hard to make them miserable?"

"I'm sorry," Maddie said. "Those guys are just creeps. Ignore them."

Jonas shook his head. "It is not only them. Since I made my new shirt, many people in the school have been unkind—everyone outside our textile arts class. No one else pushes me but they—how do you say this? Scowl and sneer. They are unfriendly. And I wonder, would I have to spend my whole life like this?"

Gwyn had thought being a geek was trouble. Being gay had to be ten times worse. "Are you gay?"

"Gwyn! I'm sorry, Jonas. You don't have to answer that. This is my brother, by the way."

"I don't mind your question, Gwyn. No, I am not gay. In Norway, before we left, I had a girlfriend. I like to sew but I play hockey too. In my school in Norway, I knew students who were gay. None of them sewed." He smiled.

"Not even the girls. But one was the best hockey player at our school and very popular, like Eric Larsen is here. If Eldar had decided to sew, other boys would have learned to sew too."

"Wow. Norway sounds like another planet," Gwyn said.

Jonas sighed. "Sometimes, I feel this way too." He turned to Maddie. "Will your parents mind that you bring me home without an invitation?"

He already had an invitation, but Maddie didn't say so, skirting the truth with skill. "I'm sure they'll be pleased to meet you. Come on, we're just a few blocks from home."

The smell of frying onions greeted them as they walked through the door. Tom was in the kitchen, making fish cakes. Gwyn was glad. He was sure none of the goons in the park had a father who'd share the cooking. It made them seem more — Norwegian.

Tom stopped to shake hands with Jonas, something he'd never done with any of their other friends. "Welcome to our home." Gwyn's father sometimes went to international conferences, so he knew how to behave with people from other countries. If people in Norway are that polite, Gwyn thought, Jonas must think we're all cavemen.

"Your mother's gone to buy milk," Tom told Maddie and Gwyn after the introductions. "When she came home, the fridge door was open and there was milk all over the floor."

"I guess somebody didn't put it away properly." Gwyn looked at the fridge so he wouldn't have to meet his father's eyes.

"I guess," Tom replied. "Try to be more careful in the future, okay?"

Gwyn wasn't happy about taking the fall for Hermit, but what else could he do?

Maddie changed the subject. "Do you want anything to drink before dinner, Jonas? There's juice."

Jonas's face lit up. "Yes, please. May I have coffee?"

"Oh, coffee." Maddie was trying not to sound surprised. Gwyn knew she had no idea how to make it.

Their father came to the rescue. "Certainly. Coffee coming right up." He went to the coffee maker on the counter and, a few minutes later, set a cup of steaming coffee in front of Jonas. Maddie got the milk and sugar.

Jonas took a sip and smiled. "This is very good coffee. Thank you." He looked puzzled. "Don't you want some?" he asked Gwyn and Maddie.

"We don't drink coffee," Gwyn explained.

"Gwyn!" Maddie said. "You make us sound so unsophisticated."

"But it's true." He turned to Jonas. "In Canada, kids hardly ever drink coffee. It's for adults. And if our mother caught us having that much caffeine, she'd have a fit."

"She's a dietitian, so what we eat is important to her."
Maddie scowled at Gwyn as if he had revealed some terrible secret about them. She rushed on. "We're really interested in tablet weaving, Jonas, because the archaeologist who found those Viking weaving tablets is a friend of my mother's." She unzipped her backpack. "Look at this, Dad. We made our weaving tablets out of cardboard today."

Tom came over, spatula in hand. "They look very ordinary."

"Anyone can make them," Jonas agreed. "But they do wonderful things. I started to learn to use them when I was just eight years old, at the Viking museum near my home. I have some sock wool here. I could show you."

Gwyn pictured Jonas unravelling old socks. "You have wool from socks?"

Jonas laughed as he reached for his backpack. "Not wool from socks, I have wool for knitting socks. It is tightly spun, so you can keep a good tension on the weaving. Ordinary wool stretches too much." He put half a dozen skeins of wool on the table—black, red, bright turquoise.

Guy colours, Gwyn thought. Maybe he was starting to think like Jonas. "You always carry wool around with you?"

Jonas laughed again. "No, not always. I thought we might start weaving in class today but we were not ready."

He took one of Maddie's weaving tablets off the table and held it up. "Once you learn to weave, Maddie, you will be able to do great things. You can even weave letters. I made a leash one Christmas, for my girlfriend in Norway, with the name of her dog woven into it."

"Wow, that's amazing. Did the Vikings do things like that?" Gwyn asked.

"Not with writing. Only more simple patterns like diamonds and arrows."

"Well, I see we have a visitor." Gwyn's mother stood in the doorway with a grocery bag.

Maddie introduced Jonas, who stood and shook Annette's hand. Gwyn waited to see if she would say something to embarrass Maddie — "Is this the boy who's being bullied?" maybe. Instead, she only said, "Have you been invited to stay for supper yet?"

Jonas beamed. "I would be honoured to share your meal. I will phone my parents to tell them I am here," and he excused himself.

While he was gone, Maddie showed the weaving tablets to her mother. Gwyn took his backpack and slipped upstairs, but Hermit was still asleep. Gwyn rummaged through his pack for something edible and came up with an apple. It had probably only been in there for a week or so — it wasn't even wrinkled. He balanced it on the top of the wardrobe and left.

Over dinner, Jonas answered questions about Norway while packing away an amazing number of fish cakes. Gwyn's father always made a double lot so he could freeze half for another meal, but this time there would hardly be any left.

When the meal was over and everyone was still talking to Jonas, Gwyn saw his chance. "I'll get the dishes," he said, gathering plates.

"Why thank you, dear!"

His mother looked so delighted that Gwyn almost felt guilty about having a secret motive. The remaining fish cakes stood on a rack near the stove. Gwyn loaded the dishwasher in record time, grabbed a paper towel, tucked two fish cakes into it and slipped along the hall, upstairs to his bedroom. Hermit was still sleeping, but the apple was gone. Gwyn found the core in his wastepaper basket. He left the fish cakes on top of his wardrobe.

"I can show you how to set up some weaving tablets now, if you like," Jonas was telling Maddie as Gwyn came back into the dining room. His parents were in the kitchen.

"Won't we need them for school?" Maddie asked.

"We made thirty cards. I can set you up with just eight and you can make a very simple weaving. That's the best way to start."

"Okay," Maddie said. "Where should we work?"

"May we look into the next room?" Jonas asked.

As they left the dining room, Maddie looked at Gwyn and raised her eyebrows. How's Hermit? she was asking. He smiled and nodded. Everything's fine. The silent conversation took only a second.

Jonas looked around the living room and shook his head. "We need a place where there are two boards. A bookcase is good."

"There's a bookcase in my bedroom. We could show you," Maddie said, and Gwyn followed them upstairs.

Maddie's bedroom, unlike Gwyn's, was almost always visitor-ready. Jonas smiled when he saw it. "Here, we can work." He pointed to the space between the headboard of Maddie's bed and the bookcase over it. "Do you have two small bungee cords?"

Gwyn resisted the urge to ask where the Vikings got their bungee cords. "I know where they are," he said instead, heading for the basement.

When he returned, Jonas was already cutting yarn, his long, delicate-looking hands working expertly. "I will set up a simple pattern and you can weave a narrow band."

Soon, Jonas was threading eight of the cardboard tablets with yarn. When they were ready, he reached for a bungee cord. "I will fix the weaving between your bed and this bookcase." The bungee cord went through the loop at the top. Finally, he stood back to admire his work. "There, that is ready." He glanced at the clock by Maddie's bed.

"But I must go now." He pushed his glasses up on his nose, a nervous gesture. "If you like, I could come back again to show you how to weave. Of course, you will be learning at school."

Gwyn realized he was giving Maddie an out, saying, You don't have to be my friend.

Maddie smiled. "I'd be glad to get some extra help with this, Jonas. Nobody in our family does any crafty stuff. Maybe you could come over on the weekend."

"I would like that very much." Jonas blushed. "And I want to thank you for saving me in the park today. You were as brave as a Viking."

Maddie shook her head and shrugged. "Oh, not really. I'll ask Dad if we can drive you home." And she was gone before he could say anything else.

Gwyn knew Maddie was only embarrassed. He didn't want Jonas to think she was rude. "She's pretty modest," he explained, then he added, "I think she could rip a guy's head off if she had to." Too late, he realized this would not be Maddie's idea of a compliment, but Jonas nodded.

"She is very brave and good. I have been hoping to find a friend like Maddie." Then, as an afterthought, he added, "I am also happy to have met you."

"Thank you," Gwyn said, trying to match Jonas's manners. He didn't really mind being an also, not where Maddie was concerned.

CHAPTER THIRTEEN

THE PROPHECY

The next day, Friday, Gwyn's lunch period came before Maddie's. When he opened the kitchen door, he found Hermit staring at a red-hot stove burner. "Hermit, you'll burn the house down!" Gwyn cried as he turned it off.

"It's so lovely to have heat and light whenever you want, like magic."

"You've got to stop playing with the appliances," Gwyn said. "I got into trouble for that milk you spilled yesterday."

"I'm sorry, Gwyn, but you canna expect me to do nothing all day. I have to have a bit of an explore when the house is empty. Tell me about the weaving in Maddie's room."

Gwyn could see there was no point in arguing. He'd try again when Maddie was home. "A friend of my mother's found some Viking weaving tablets over the summer—"

Hermit cut him off. "Weaving tablets? Belonging to Vikings? How do you know?"

Gwyn explained about the Viking site at L'Anse aux Meadows, opening a can of tuna as he talked. "It's the only Viking site in North America. They found it in the 1960s, when an archaeologist and her husband sailed down the northeast coast of Canada, looking for landscapes described in the Norse sagas. Everywhere they stopped, they asked if anyone knew of a place that looked like it might have been a settlement. When they came to L'Anse aux Meadows on the Great Northern Peninsula, a man took them to the Viking site. It was all grown over, but when they started to dig they found houses and artifacts."

Hermit nodded. "Daniel was sure they'd find it one day. He imagined it closer to St. John's, though. And these weaving tablets, are they still up there?"

Gwyn shook his head. "I don't think so. They're going on display here soon, so they must be in town some-where."

"This is all very good," Hermit replied. "Very good indeed. Things are finally falling into place. After all these years. I'd almost given up hope."

Before Gwyn could ask what he meant, Maddie arrived.

"Hermit's really excited about those Viking weaving tablets," Gwyn told her.

Hermit snorted. "They're no Viking weaving tablets, laddie. Those tablets were stolen from your ancestors."

"Did Gwyn tell you about Jonas?" Maddie asked. Gwyn shook his head. "Oh, well, a Norwegian student came here last night —"

Hermit's crest flattened against his skull. "Norse? A Viking? I canna believe you let a Viking into my house!" It sounded like "*ma hoose.*"

Gwyn laughed. "Excuse me? I think this is our house."

"Of course it is. You're dragon keepers. Your house is my house. And I'll no have Vikings in it."

Gwyn couldn't believe the nerve of this little guy. His house! No Vikings! He opened his mouth to argue, but Maddie cut him off with a warning look.

"Now, Hermit," she said, "don't be like that. Jonas is nothing like a Viking. The Scandinavians are very civilized now. So much has changed." She shook her head. "Where do we start?" she asked Gwyn.

"Where we always do. Hermit, you can read, can't you?"

Hermit nodded. "Aye, learning to read was very popular during the Reformation."

Gwyn wasn't sure when that was, but it was the answer he'd hoped for. "When we've finished eating, I'll take you upstairs. It's time you were introduced to the computer. That will help keep you busy while we're gone, too." He put a tuna sandwich on a plate on the floor for Hermit and two more on the table. Maddie sat down.

"That was lovely," Hermit said as they finished eating. "Tell me," he added, "do you know where the prophecy is?"

Gwyn exchanged a look with Maddie. "The what?"

Hermit sighed. "The prophecy. About the lifting of the curse that keeps the dragons hidden. When Madoca took me away from our ancestral home, she went to a monastery and asked them to write it down so it wouldn'a be forgotten. They were Picts, those monks, so she told them everything she knew about the dragons, hoping they might write that down, too. The prophecy has been passed from generation to generation and carefully recopied ever since. Daniel carried it with him when we crossed the sea. Dinna tell me it's been thrown away."

"Oh, that! Of course not. It's right here in the house."

"Thank heaven. We can sit down with it and I'll explain everything to you."

"We'll ask Dad to let us look at it," Gwyn said.

"Good. Your father can hear the story too," Hermit replied. "It's time we met."

A heavy silence settled on the room.

Maddie finally spoke. "Hermit, you don't understand. If our father saw you, he might want to study you."

Hermit nodded. "I'd be pleased to be studied."

Gwyn remembered the books he'd read about Victorian naturalists. "People don't just use magnifying glasses now. They'd probably keep you in a lab. You'd be a prisoner, more or less."

Hermit drew back. "I must have my freedom, laddie. Being shut up in this house is bad enough. I've a mission to accomplish. Everything depends upon it. Everything."

"Then we have to keep you a secret," Maddie said.

Gwyn nodded. He had no idea what Hermit was talking about, but anything that convinced him to stay hidden was good. "Tonight, I'll ask Dad if we can see the manuscript."

"Maybe we could show it to Jonas when he comes to teach me how to use the weaving tablets," Maddie added.

"Your Viking friend is going to teach you to weave?" Hermit asked. Gwyn waited for him to get upset about Jonas again, but instead he just nodded. "Learn to use the weaving tablets, Maddie. Madoca was a skillful weaver and you have her blood in your veins. I'm sure you'll do well."

"I hope you're right, Hermit," Maddie replied.

"In the meantime," Gwyn said, "promise us you'll stay out of sight, up on the top floor in my room." He glanced over to the timetable on the fridge. "Dad doesn't teach on Friday afternoons and he might come home any time."

"Let's get you upstairs now," Maddie said. "We'll show

you how to use the computer and you can spend the afternoon catching up on the world."

Hermit climbed onto her shoulders. "I canna stay locked up in here forever, though. You'll have to take me out sometime so I can stretch my wings." It wasn't a question.

"We'll figure out something," Maddie replied before Gwyn could protest.

When they sat Hermit at the computer, they found the touch pad was too hard for him to handle. "Good thing this is just Dad's old laptop," Gwyn said, eyeing the scratches the dragon's sharp claws had made.

"I think I have a pocket mouse," Maddie said.

"I'll have no rodents in this room! It's messy enough as it is," Hermit cried.

"You can handle this one." Maddie was laughing as she disappeared.

"You'll see when she comes back," Gwyn said. He opened a page. "Here's a search engine." He showed Hermit how to use it.

"How do all they pages fit into that wee picture box?" Hermit asked after a while.

"It's hard to explain. Do you know about the telephone?"

"Oh, aye. Daniel was very interested in it. He was sure people in Newfoundland would have them one day."

"Good. Well, it's something like that. My computer can hook up to a network of computers all over the world, sort of like it's making a telephone call. Most of what you see on the screen isn't inside this computer at all."

Hermit shook his head. "I thought Daniel was being fanciful."

"No, he was right. Look, I've bookmarked some links to online encyclopedias and science journals."

Maddie returned with the pocket mouse and Gwyn showed Hermit how to click on hypertext links to follow a topic. Then he noticed his clock. "Yikes. I'm going to be late for class. You're all set. Go crazy, little guy."

The dragon only nodded, already mesmerized by the computer screen.

All afternoon, Gwyn wondered what would happen if his father came home early, but the car was not in the driveway after school. Maddie's coat and backpack were already in the hall by the door and Gwyn found her with Hermit at his computer.

"Oh, good. We've been waiting for you," Hermit said. Maddie had taken over at the keyboard. "Show him."

"This is where our ancestors came from, hundreds of years ago." Maddie brought up pictures of a green, tree-less landscape. "A group of islands called Orkney, off the north coast of Scotland."

"Let him see the map, Maddie," Hermit urged.

Maddie brought up a map of many islands, all different sizes. "Sunny would love this place, Gwyn. The archaeology goes back thousands of years. Look." She opened a map that showed a long neck of land between two lakes, then some photos of stone circles.

"These stone circles were very important to your people," Hermit said. "They were magic then. When I was born, we thought they were given to us by the gods, but today I've learned they were built by people who lived five thousand years ago. That fascinates me because your people also believed that the dragons were given to them by the gods."

"You think the people who built those stone circles tamed the dragons?" Maddie asked.

"Maybe. We may never know." Hermit shook his head. "But in the past century people have learned other things I thought we'd never know. It's a very good sign."

"Sign of what?" Gwyn asked.

"It's a long story and you may find it hard to believe. It's better if I start with the prophecy and explain from there."

Gwyn wondered what Hermit would call hard to believe. The little dragon yawned. "Have you been here all afternoon?" Gwyn asked.

"Aye, it's a handy wee tool, this."

"Yes, but you've worn yourself out," Maddie said. "Time for a nap."

"I'd like to go outside tomorrow if the weather isn'a too bad," Hermit said as Maddie boosted him into his lair.

Maddie didn't argue. "We'll see what we can do. Jonas is coming over in the afternoon."

"I could get up early and pretend to go birding," Gwyn added.

∘ ∘ ∘

That night after supper, Maddie asked her father about the manuscript. "I haven't seen it since I was little," she said. "And Gwyn's research has got us interested in the past. Do you think we could have a look?"

Tom went to his study and returned with it a moment later. "I suppose I should have given it to the Provincial Archives with the other papers. For some reason, I just like to know it's near. Sunny nearly had a fit when she realized we had something this old. She gave us an acid-free folder to keep it in. Be careful. I wish I had time to look at it with you but I'm on the examining committee for a doctoral thesis that's just been submitted. My weekend is pretty much shot."

Gwyn was sorry his father had so much work, but glad they could show the old manuscript to Hermit without him. He'd been worried about that. As he carried the folder upstairs, carefully using both hands, it hummed, almost like the key, but it was quieter and more musical. The magic filled him with a powerful anticipation.

Maddie opened the folder when he laid it on his desk. "Hermit," she whispered, "we've got it."

"Not much worse for wear, I see." The dragon clambered down, touching the floor lightly before springing onto Gwyn's bed.

"How old is it?" Gwyn asked.

"This one was copied out in the early 1600s. By that time, the printing press had changed everything and your ancestor, John Calvin MacLeish, was afraid people might lose the skill of writing since they had machines to do it for them. Let me have a look."

Gwyn turned on his desk lamp.

"Ah," Hermit said. "This takes me back. Now, events are falling into place and I'll need your help, so you must know the story to understand Madoca's prophecy. The Vikings came to Orkney around the time I hatched, and everything went awry. They'd already killed most of the dragons in the Norselands and they would have killed the dragons on Orkney, too, but your ancestor, Madoca, opened a magic place inside one of the stone circles and sent all the dragons into it. I was supposed to go as well but I was just a wee thing, only a few months old, and I had no way of understanding what was happening. At the

last moment, I turned back to Madoca, the magic faded
and I was trapped here, the last of my kind."

"So this old witch put a spell on you, to keep you alive
all this time?" Gwyn asked.

Hermit ground his beak, making that scratchy noise
that was dragon laughter. "That old witch was about
the age of Maddie when she worked her magic, laddie.
Madoca made a counter-spell, and I was part of it. That's
what's kept me from growing to full size all this time. But
it wasn'a just to keep me alive. Read it."

"Wow, this is barely English," Gwyn said.

"You're lucky it's English at all," Hermit replied.
"Before, it was always written in Latin."

Maddie began to read. "*Longe ago, in the darkest hour
when Viking raiders rained upon the lande like locust, all the
dragons fled into the safety of the ring, save one. We are the people
of the dragon and shall be so long as the curyse remaines. In the
place where the sun does first cast lyhte'* — oh, light — '*upon the
undiscovered worlde, there shall the curyse be unmade. Then shall
men once mor knowe the dragons are as fryends to mankynd and
the great balance be made mend.*'"

"Well, that's as clear as mud," Gwyn grumbled. He'd
expected some great revelation.

"The place where the sun first casts its light on the
undiscovered world. That's Newfoundland! Is that why
Daniel brought you here?" Maddie asked.

"Clever lass. Aye, it is," Hermit replied.

"Tell us about the curse," she continued.

"A powerful Viking seer was so angry when Madoca saved the dragons that he wove a curse. That's why your people disappeared and all their lore with them. That's why no one knows about the dragons."

"But you're still here," Maddie said.

"Aye," Hermit said. "It's my mission to finally complete the counter-spell that will undo the curse. Daniel and I came here so we could do that, and then we waited." Hermit paused with great, deliberate drama.

"For what?" Gwyn asked.

"For the weaving tablets! The seer who cursed your people stole them from Madoca. They belong to you." Hermit's eyes shone. "Together, we must claim them so we can unweave the curse."

"Hermit," Gwyn cried, "do you have any idea how valuable those tablets are?"

"Of course I do, laddie. They're priceless."

"We'll never be allowed to touch them," Maddie said. "They belong to the province now."

This didn't faze Hermit. "I've waited more than a thousand years. Do you think I'd let a little thing like that bother me? You learn how to weave, Maddie. That's all you need do for now. We'll get those weaving tablets if it takes the rest of your lives."

Gwyn noticed that Hermit took it for granted he and Maddie would be okay with this.

Maddie closed the folder over the manuscript. "I'll take this back to Dad." She gave Gwyn a look, warning him not to argue, but Gwyn already knew that. If Hermit got excited and started to yell, their father might hear. Better to change the subject.

"Let's look at the computer again," he said when Maddie left. "I'll show you some pterosaurs."

"Look at them!" Hermit cried after a few minutes. "So many different kinds." He sopped up information like a sponge. For someone with Victorian ideas about science, Gwyn noticed, Hermit accepted new concepts quickly. He was like a little learning machine. No, better. No machine was that smart. By bedtime, Gwyn had new respect for Hermit. As for the crazy, impossible idea of using Sunny's weaving tablets to undo a curse, they'd just have to talk him out of that.

CHAPTER FOURTEEN

AROUND THE LAKE

Gwyn was snowboarding down hills as slick as satin, fast and faster, the board responding perfectly, the wind like a jolt of caffeine. Then, suddenly the snow shifted as Gwyn felt himself tipping into an avalanche. He grasped at nothing as he fell — and found he was clutching at his blankets as they slid off the bed.

Hermit's saucer eyes blinked from just beyond the mattress. "Time to be away, laddie. The sun's almost up."

Gwyn glanced at his clock. It was already eight and almost light outside. He tiptoed to the hall and looked down-stairs. The bathroom door was shut and there was someone in the shower, probably his mother, who was always first up on the weekends. He began to scoop dirty clothes off the dresser and floor. "Bring me the fleece throw Maddie gave you." Hermit threw him a reproachful look. "Please," Gwyn added.

"I'm pleased to see you finally give this room a good tidying," Hermit said after he placed the small blanket on the bed.

Gwyn didn't have the heart to tell him the laundry basket was the safest way to get the little dragon through the house without being seen. When the basket was full, Gwyn picked it up. "Climb on and I'll cover you with the fleece." Hermit did.

Gwyn went down through the kitchen, into the basement. "This should make Mom happy. I'm supposed to do my own laundry but I hardly ever do."

Hermit eyed the big white washing machine as it filled with water. "What do all the laundresses do for a living now, I wonder?"

"Laundresses?"

"Aye, the women who make their living by taking in laundry."

"Oh. They must have other jobs now."

"Working with computers?" Hermit asked.

Gwyn wasn't sure. "Maybe. What would you like for breakfast?"

"Porridge! I'd love a muckle great bowl of steaming porridge."

"Oatmeal? I can probably do that," Gwyn replied. "You stay here."

Of course they had oatmeal. And Cream of Wheat and Red River. Gwyn's mother was always trying to get them to eat hot cereal. Now, as he read the instructions on the package, Gwyn wished he'd paid more attention.

"Oatmeal! Look at you!" Annette smiled.

Gwyn almost dropped the box. "I'm going around the lake and I thought I should eat a hot breakfast," he mumbled. This felt like pleasing her under false pretenses. She was so happy to show him how to make the oatmeal.

"I'm off," she said as soon as the bowl was in the microwave. "Meeting Sunny for brunch and then we're going shopping. She wants to find the perfect outfit for the opening of that Viking exhibit. We'll probably go through every dress shop in the city —" There was a loud crash in the basement. Gwyn froze. "What could that be?" Annette asked.

"I put some laundry in. Maybe the load was unbalanced and the machine started rocking."

"We'd better check."

"No!" Gwyn cried before he could stop himself. "I mean, no, it's okay, you go on. I'll check."

Annette shook her head. "I want to see for myself. So many odd things have been happening around this house lately. Sometimes the lamp on my bedside table is on when I come home though I'm sure I turned it off in the morning."

The bottom fell out of Gwyn's stomach as he followed his mother down the basement stairs. The box of flashlights was lying on its side on top of the washer. Hermit sat on the shelf where the box had been, in plain sight. Gwyn waited for his mother's scream.

"Well, there's the answer," Annette said, walking over to the box. "I wonder how that happened?" She was face to face with Hermit now.

Gwyn took a deep breath. "Dad thought the power might go out last week, so we charged the flashlights. I guess I didn't put the box back properly." Past his mother's shoulder, he glared at Hermit. That box had been safely stowed.

"Well, let's make sure we do it right this time. This house is starting to unnerve me." She picked up the box and shoved it toward Hermit.

"Be careful!" Gwyn cried. Hermit took off, flying right over their heads.

Annette laughed as she turned to him. The box was back on the shelf. "Gwyn, I'm always careful. Did you feel a draft? We may have to get new windows for this basement. I've got to run now, Sunny will be waiting." She walked right past Hermit on her way to the stairs.

Gwyn had to prop himself up with the washing machine, his heart pounding as if he'd just run a sprint.

"Sorry," Hermit said. "Curiosity got the better of me. Do I smell porridge?"

He was not happy about eating in the basement. Gwyn put extra brown sugar on the oatmeal to make up for that. Then he got his clothes into the dryer, tidied the breakfast dishes and was out of the house with Hermit before anyone else stirred.

"What a beautiful day!" Hermit exclaimed when they finally slipped out the side door. Gwyn was glad his parents' bedroom was on the other side of the house. Hermit could be pretty loud.

Weak winter sun filled the blue sky, but the temperature had dropped again. "Are you going to be warm enough?" Gwyn asked.

"Oh, aye. Flying keeps me warm. I'll be hungry by the time we finish, though. It's been so many years since I had a good glide."

There was longing in his voice and Gwyn realized he was only hanging back to be polite.

"Remember Quidi Vidi Lake?" he asked.

"Oh, aye. We called it 'the pond.'"

Gwyn smiled. "We still do. It's that way." He pointed down the street. "I'll meet you there. Watch out for all the overhead wires."

"Woo hoo!" Hermit cried as he launched into the air, sounding like a little kid. He cleared the trees around the house and circled before heading straight for the lake. Gwyn stood with his mouth open. Hermit's flying was amazing. He could stop and hover like a tern. Gwyn tried to imagine the sky full of such creatures as once, millions of years ago, these skies had been.

Too bad *I* can't fly, Gwyn thought as he looked down. Everything was covered in new ice, as smooth as glass. He ducked back into the house to get a pair of ice-grippers for his boots.

It took about twenty minutes to walk to the lake. Passing the old wooden houses of the east end, some almost unchanged since Daniel's day, Gwyn had time to think. It wasn't hard to believe that the Vikings had wanted to destroy the dragons. People were cruel to birds even now, and dragons looked a lot stranger than birds. Gwyn shook his head. People killed animals that scared them. Hermit had somehow survived and he was convinced he had a mission to do—what? Restore the dragons to the world? How would that work? People would just start killing them all over again, or they'd stick them in labs and zoos. It would be a nightmare.

Gwyn stopped at the edge of the lake and took out his field glasses. Hermit hovered in the sky, almost unmoving, like a kite with a long tail. His open wings outlined his small body in translucent triangles of skin that reached from his wing tips to his back legs. His large head turned from side to side as he took in the sights. He was so buoyant, he looked lighter than air. He swooped away to circle the lake. The gulls mistook him for a large predator and they took flight.

A man noticed Gwyn with his field glasses. "What's bothering them?"

Gwyn shrugged. "Do you see anything?" The man shook his head.

Gwyn walked to the mouth of the Virginia River, found a dry bench and settled down to wait. Hermit swooped and soared until a distant rumble filled the sky. This was a flight path to the airport, one that gave travellers a fabulous view of the city. The plane was high, no danger to Hermit, but suddenly he hurtled out of the sky, aiming for Gwyn like a missile.

"What's that terrible machine?" Hermit asked, crouching on the bench beside him.

"I'm sorry. I should have warned you about airplanes and helicopters. Climb up and I'll explain while we walk around the lake."

As Hermit scrambled up, Gwyn realized the dragon was shivering, maybe from so much exercise, maybe from fright. Gwyn pulled his warm wool scarf from inside his coat. "Let's wrap this around you," he said. As they walked, he gave Hermit a quick overview of air travel, speaking quietly. He tried to pause whenever a runner or walker came their way, but there were bends in the trail, and more than once people gave him funny looks as they passed. Did they think he was talking to himself? Or maybe his scarf looked like it was hanging in mid-air.

"So people just climb into these machines and fly?" Hermit asked when he'd finished.

"Well, there's a pilot to fly for them, but yes. Don't go too high and you'll be safe. The airport is over that way." Gwyn pointed past far hills. "Be sure to keep away."

Hermit had stopped shivering, but he huddled against the back of Gwyn's neck. "How long would it take to cross the ocean in one of they contraptions?" he finally asked.

"Not long. People do it overnight."

"Overnight! It took two weeks when Daniel and I came to Newfoundland. We argued the whole time about whether I could go off flying. Daniel was afraid I'd lose track of the ship and get lost out at sea."

Gwyn smiled. "Who won?"

"We compromised. I could make short flights as long as Daniel kept me in his sights. No flying without his permission. But, by then, everyone on the ship was convinced Daniel was a madman, yelling at himself in his cabin. It made for a very odd voyage."

"And that's why people thought Daniel was so strange."

"Aye, and that was why he never married. He always said he couldn'a expect a woman to believe in something invisible. I'd tell him Christians believe in any number of things they canna see and that would set us off again. He wanted to bring Hamish to Newfoundland to become the next dragon keeper but he had no idea how Agatha was going to accept my story."

"Do you think James ever tried to tell her about you?"

"We were hoping he had. It would have made the task easier for Daniel. What sort of person was Hamish? Do you know?"

Gwyn told Hermit about his great-grandfather, the respected doctor. "There's an entry in the *Encyclopedia of Newfoundland*. We can look it up tonight," he concluded.

"Sounds as if he would have made a fine dragon keeper," Hermit said.

They both fell silent. Gwyn imagined Hermit was remembering Daniel and James. For his part, Gwyn was trying to picture the future with Hermit. Would people think he was crazy, too? It seemed inevitable.

There were more people on the trail now, so they didn't speak again. When they reached the bridge where the Rennie's River flowed into the lake, Gwyn took the river trail home. Hermit seemed to change, still too light to be a burden, but distinctly heavier. Finally, the little dragon's beak came to rest on Gwyn's shoulder.

"Something's wrong," Hermit murmured. "I canna quite place it, but it's as if there's a pane of glass between the world and myself. The dragons have always been able to connect to the web of life, but now I find it so difficult."

Was Hermit sick? Gwyn almost panicked at the idea. "You probably got too much exercise."

Hermit only nodded. He was growing limp.

"We're almost home," Gwyn said.

CHAPTER FIFTEEN

MADDIE LEARNS TO WEAVE

Gwyn's mother was still out when they got home, and his father was locked away, reading the new thesis, so it was easy to sneak Hermit upstairs. Gwyn left him on the bed in a nest of blankets, then found Maddie in the kitchen, reading a novel and munching toast.

"I took Hermit out flying and now he seems sick," Gwyn whispered.

"Oh no. He's probably worn out. Let's feed him a good lunch. Dad took out a container of Mom's chicken soup."

Gwyn thought of the warm fleece blanket in the dryer. "Okay, I'll get my laundry."

Maddie raised an eyebrow. "You did laundry?"

Gwyn told Maddie what had happened when Hermit

knocked over the box in the basement. "So he really is invisible," he concluded.

Maddie glanced to the closed door of their father's study. "Not to everyone."

Gwyn returned with his clean laundry just as Maddie took a steaming bowl of soup from the microwave. Upstairs, they found Hermit slumped on the bed.

"Come on, little guy," Gwyn said. "Chicken soup."

Hermit's eyes flew open. "With noodles?"

Maddie set the bowl down on Gwyn's desk, then lifted Hermit over to it. She frowned, and Gwyn knew she felt what he had—Hermit seemed unwell. But she kept her voice cheerful.

"There you go, Hermit. Mom's chicken soup can cure anything."

Gwyn found himself wishing that old family joke were true. He pushed the clean fleece up on top of the wardrobe, then made his bed to keep busy. He couldn't sit still.

"That was a lovely bowl of soup," Hermit said after he'd slurped up the last noodle.

"How do you feel?" Maddie asked.

"Better, but I need sleep." He shook his head. "I canna believe the world has changed so much in just over a hundred years. Everything feels off balance."

As they boosted him into his lair, the doorbell rang. "That'll be Jonas," Maddie said, and they went to let him in.

"So, are you ready to become a Viking weaver?" Jonas smiled as he shucked off his coat and boots.

Gwyn glanced up the stairs, half expecting Hermit to come storming down. "Maybe Maddie's a Pictish weaver," he said.

Jonas looked confused.

"Don't worry, it's sort of a family joke." Maddie shook her head as they climbed the stairs to her bedroom.

Jonas opened his backpack and took out a flat piece of wood with grooves on either end and a stick that looked like a ruler. "We will wind the weft wool around this shuttle, then, you can weave." He picked up the stick. "And this to make the rows neat." He showed Maddie how to turn the tablets and wove the first few lines to start her off, carefully pushing each row down with the stick before weaving a new one. But, as soon as he handed the shuttle to Maddie, the weaving went funny. After a moment, Jonas said, "You're pulling too tightly. See how the band bunches in?" Soon after, Jonas added, "You've missed a thread in that line. See how it makes a flaw in the pattern?"

Gwyn had assumed Maddie would be a brilliant weaver. Hermit had said as much, and she did everything well. But it wasn't working out that way.

After a few minutes she said, "This looks terrible. Could we start over?"

Jonas smiled. "It takes a long time to set up a weaving. It's better to make all your mistakes in this piece. Then, when you do a perfect weaving, you can compare them and laugh."

Though he was patient and encouraging, Maddie got more and more flustered. She wasn't used to being bad at anything. "I thought it would be easier," she said at last. The band she'd woven pulled in at either side and the pattern was full of flaws.

"Some people find it harder than others." Jonas still sounded encouraging.

"I bet you didn't," Maddie replied. "I bet your first weaving looked a lot better than this."

Jonas said nothing, and Gwyn knew she was right.

Maddie gave a weak laugh, trying not to show how much it bothered her. "It's a good thing I've got you to give me extra help. Let's have some lunch."

The smell of chicken soup brought Tom out of his study with the dazed look of someone who'd been off in another world.

"Interesting thesis?" Gwyn asked.

He nodded. "The student is refining a new technique for creating more copies of DNA from smaller samples."

"How small?"

"Small enough to be collected from a fingerprint."

"Wow. You could identify someone's DNA from a fingerprint?" They fell into a lively discussion of what that might mean for police work, then for crime novels. Maddie and Jonas were just as interested as Gwyn, and somehow lunch was over.

"I'd better get back to work if I want some free time tomorrow," Tom said, gathering up the dishes. "When are you going to show us your weaving, Maddie?"

Maddie made a face. "Not yet. This one's a bit of a disaster."

"I'm sure many people in our class will have the same problems," Jonas added quickly.

"I'm not," Maddie said as she rose from the table. "They have talent. I'm just a jock who landed in that class by accident. I really enjoy it, but I don't think I'll ever be good at textile arts." She sounded certain.

"I think it is too soon to tell," Jonas replied.

The front door flew open and Annette came into the kitchen with Sunny, dumping bags of groceries on the floor. "Oh, excellent. Jonas," Annette said, "I'm glad you're here. I'd like you to meet my friend, Dr. Sunny Goodman. Sunny is the archaeologist who found the Viking weaving tablets this summer. Sunny, this is Maddie's friend who weaves."

The way Sunny lunged at Jonas, Gwyn was surprised she didn't knock him over. "I'm so happy to meet you. We can talk more over supper."

"Supper?" Jonas looked dazed.

"Yes, please stay for supper," Annette said. "I'm going to teach Sunny to make spanakopita. We've been meaning to do this for ages. Do you like Greek food, Jonas?"

"It would give me pleasure to stay for dinner," Jonas replied.

"Fabulous," Sunny said. "This is going to be so much fun."

Back in Maddie's room, the weaving sat untouched as Jonas and Maddie started talking about books Gwyn hadn't read and people he didn't know. "I think I'll work on my Heritage Fair project," Gwyn said after a few minutes, meaning he was going to check on Hermit.

But Hermit was not visible in his lair. Best to let him sleep, Gwyn thought. He pulled his notes from the Mews Annex out of his backpack to distract himself. The Heritage Fair was only a few weeks away. He typed a heading: "Daniel Rae, A Victorian Naturalist Examines the Nature of Flight." He paused to admire his work. Pretty good so far. Brilliant, even. He changed the font to something fancy, Balmoral it was called. *Daniel Rae, A Victorian Naturalist Examines the Nature of Flight.* He took the font up to thirty-six points, centred it and added a colon:

Daniel Rae:
A Victorian Naturalist Examines the Nature of Flight

That would look great on a poster. There. A perfect start. What's spanakopita? he wondered. He pushed his chair away from the desk. Maybe he could watch his mother cook.

"That's a very nice title. Now, you need an essay to go with it." Hermit looked normal again as he climbed down from his lair. "Let me see your notes."

"I thought I'd go down to the kitchen. The archaeologist who found the tablets is here."

Hermit stopped him with a glare. "After all these years, laddie, I know an excuse to avoid doing lessons when I hear one. Let's get to work."

Hermit made Gwyn do all the work, and he was a real stickler for grammar and spelling, too. Before long, Gwyn found he had the final draft of a two-page biography of Daniel Rae.

"Dinner, Gwyn," Maddie called from downstairs.

"I'll bring you something to eat as soon as I can," he promised Hermit as he left.

"We'll be downstairs," Maddie called to Jonas, who was in the bathroom. "How's our little friend?" she whispered to Gwyn on the stairs.

"Fine, much better."

"What happened, do you think?"

Gwyn shook his head.

When everyone was seated, Sunny brought the spanakopita to the table with a flourish. "TA-DA!"

"Wow," Maddie said. "It looks terrific."

She wasn't just being polite. The pan of golden, flaky pastry made Gwyn's stomach growl.

"I never make this," Annette said, looking directly at Gwyn, "because a certain person in our family has a strong aversion to spinach. But, if any dish could convert a spinach hater, this is it. Just try some, Gwyn," she urged.

After Gwyn finished his first forkful, he smiled. "Okay, you win."

Everyone praised the spanakopita, the Greek salad, the homemade pita bread and dips that Annette and Sunny had made that afternoon. "This is better than publishing a paper," Sunny said. "Rave reviews! Now, tell me, how's the weaving?"

Jonas spoke before Maddie could. "Maddie is learning. It's hard for someone who is a complete beginner. People who knit or weave on a loom would find it easier."

"I bet you're a terrific teacher, Jonas," Sunny replied. "I've been talking to your textile arts teacher about putting on a display to go with our exhibit at The Rooms. We'd like to show examples of the work from your class. Do you think you could teach a workshop, too? We have funds for materials and a small fee for you."

Jonas smiled. "This would make me very happy."

"Did people in other places use weaving tablets in the past?" Maddie asked.

Gwyn's ears perked up. He knew why she was asking.

"Oh yes," Sunny replied. "All over Asia and North Africa and Europe—from Iceland to China, probably for thousands of years. There are ancient Egyptian statues that seem to have tablet-woven bands on their clothing."

"And the Picts?" Maddie asked. "I found this pamphlet, written by one of our ancestors, Daniel Rae's father, I think, about the Picts."

"Yes!" Sunny said. "It's funny you should ask. I've read everything I can find about tablet weaving since last summer, and there's a famous piece of clothing, the Orkney Hood, it's called. People used to think it was made by the Vikings. Now we know it was made before the Vikings arrived. It was probably woven by Picts."

"Do you know much about the Picts?" Maddie asked. "Alexander Rae seemed to think we're descended from them."

Sunny laughed. "Oh, he probably had a case of Pictomania."

"What's that?" Gwyn asked.

"One of my first archaeology professors was a Scot, Dr. Anderson. He would warn us about this dreaded disease, Pictomania, that seems to affect people who take an interest in Scottish archaeology. Dr. Anderson had a whole lecture about the Picts and all the odd ideas people have projected onto them."

"Why would they do that?" Tom asked.

"Because we know so little about them. All the other people who lived around the same time are better documented. We know the Picts used the same everyday objects as other peoples, but they put unique designs on their jewellery and the stone monuments they carved, and they had different burial customs. And that's all we know. Dr. Anderson used to say, 'It's as if the slate of history has been wiped clean where the Picts are concerned.'"

"But isn't that true of everyone who lived in the distant past?" Tom asked.

"Distant past, yes," Sunny replied. "Go back a few thousand years and we know virtually nothing. But the Picts didn't live in the distant past. They disappeared in the ninth century, Early Historic we call that now. We really should know more about them than we do."

"But Sunny, what do you mean 'disappeared'?" Annette asked. "People don't just disappear."

"The Picts did," Sunny insisted. "They just ceased to exist as a people in Scotland. Gone. Vanished."

Sunny sounded eerily like Hermit. It was so weird that Gwyn shivered.

"So what happened? Did invaders take over their lands?" Tom asked.

"Not really. Invasion isn't as common as people think. The Vikings did take over Orkney completely, but in the rest of Scotland, the Picts just seem to have blended in with the people around them."

"It's chilling to think a whole culture could disappear like that, isn't it?" Annette said.

"Chilling enough to require a good strong cup of coffee and some cake," Tom replied, rising from the table. "I have to admit, I'm glad that didn't happen to anyone we know."

Gwyn stole a glance at Maddie, who had been silent through this conversation. For once, their father was wrong. It *had* happened to someone they knew.

CHAPTER SIXTEEN

A Heated Debate on the Nature of Dragons

On Monday, after school, Gwyn and Maddie walked to the Mews Annex huddled into their coats. The inside of Gwyn's nose froze slightly every time he breathed in, but he didn't mind because the sun was shining. A high-pressure system had swept this cold air down from the Arctic, clearing all the winter clouds away. The sky was a pure, powdery blue and snowflakes glittered as they fell in the sunshine. Snowflakes? Gwyn looked up. A few puffy clouds floated far off to the north and the wind was blowing from that direction. It was possible, just barely. He caught a snowflake on his black mitten, one of those perfect no-two-alike discs, the kind that hardly ever hit the ground in one piece, and held it out to Maddie.

"Snow? Today?" She looked up at the snowflake-spangled breeze. "It's like magic."

Gwyn nodded. "It is, and how many people will see it? You know, I walked around the lake on Saturday with Hermit on my shoulder. Even when the gulls went crazy, even with my scarf floating six inches above my collar, people hardly noticed. They could go through their whole lives with magic all around them and never know it."

Maddie nodded. "Not us, though. Have you thought about what life's going to be like, looking after Hermit?"

"A little. No wonder everyone thought Daniel was such an oddball."

"It's not going to be easy."

Gwyn tried to think of a reason to contradict her. "I don't know," he said at last. "Maybe we can take turns." He really needed to change the subject. It was just too big. "In history class today, Mr. Banfield asked how many of us were planning to present projects at the Heritage Fair. Most were kids you'd expect, like Bunny Larsen, but Tyler Cull put up his hand."

Maddie laughed. "Really? Tyler Cull, historian. I wonder what his project's about."

"Maybe a history of bullying. But he's leaving me

alone. Maddie, are the guys at your school bothering Jonas now?"

"I don't think so. Why?"

"I wonder about that. You just ordered those goons to back off and they did. Maybe it's—like Hermit. You know?"

"You think *I'm* magic?" Maddie shook her head. "Gwyn, that's crazy."

"Maybe. So much of this is crazy. Snow falls on a sunny day, we have an ancient dragon living in our house and those people, the Picts, they just disappeared—*poof*!"

"That wasn't magic. Sunny explained it."

"Well, Hermit said it was, and everything else Sunny said fits with Hermit's story. Now Sunny's found those tablets and Hermit says *they're* magic. And that ancestor of ours, what was her name?"

"Madoca."

"Yeah, her. She was magic, so maybe you are, too."

Maddie laughed. "Gwyn, if I'm magic, why can't I stop those girls on the soccer team from being so mean to me?"

"Did you ever order them to leave you alone? The way you did for me and Jonas?"

"Of course not." Maddie was silent for a moment, then she said, "You think that would work?"

"If I were you, I'd give it a try."

Maddie shook her head. "I don't know, Gwyn. Next thing, you'll be stealing those weaving tablets. All this talk of magic makes me dizzy. Is this your last day at the annex?"

"If the photos are ready. The Heritage Fair is only two weeks away. Hermit helped me write a bio of Daniel on the weekend. He's a bit of a slave-driver. He offered to help me with my Latin, too. He didn't believe me when I told him we don't study it."

Maddie laughed.

Inside the Colonial Building, they could hear loud music wafting out of the Mews Annex before they opened the door.

"Ah, there you are," Dr. Mews said. "This is your last day, isn't it? I thought we'd celebrate with a bit of music."

Brassy music blared while people half sang, half yelled at one another. Gwyn vaguely recognized it as opera. He wanted to ask Dr. Mews to turn it off, but that might be rude. A large envelope sat on the desk Gwyn had used over the past few weeks. His name was on the label. "The photos?" he asked.

Dr. Mews smiled. "They arrived about an hour ago. Have a look."

Gwyn took a photo from the envelope and there was Daniel, posed at his desk. Now that it was enlarged, Gwyn could see Hermit, sitting on a bookshelf behind

Daniel between two stuffed birds, his eyes bright with mischief. Maddie burst out laughing.

"What's so funny?" Dr. Mews asked.

"Oh, it's just that he looks so much like our father," Gwyn covered for her.

Maddie peered into the envelope, pulling out another photo. She had asked for a picture of downtown St. John's, showing the Kirk and the harbour beyond, the now-demolished buildings still beside it.

"That was such a lovely piece of land," Dr. Mews grumbled. "What is it now? A parking lot full of gravel and broken glass. What else have you got?"

The other photos all had something to do with birds. There were birds by water and in trees, photographs of an egg collection, even a few of children holding chickens. "I wish Daniel had taken some pictures of birds in flight," Gwyn said. "That's what my project is about."

Dr. Mews shook his head. "Impossible in those days. The exposure time was too long to capture anything moving." He pointed to a photograph of a boy holding a chicken. The bird was just a blur of feathers. "See? If something moved while the camera's lens was open, the image was ruined."

"Maybe you could take some photos yourself to go with the project," Maddie suggested.

Gwyn nodded. The music in the background reached a crescendo. One of the singers had a voice so low, it was almost painful. Gwyn's curiosity got the better of him. "Dr. Mews, what is that music?"

Dr. Mews smiled. "It's Wagner's opera *Siegfried*. Do you like it?"

Gwyn dodged the question. "That guy has a really low voice, doesn't he?"

"That's a basso profundo. He's playing the dragon, Fafner."

"Dragons don't sound anything like that," Gwyn muttered.

Dr. Mews didn't hear him over the music. "It's a great story, full of adventure and magic," he continued with enthusiasm. "In this scene, Siegfried, the hero, slays the evil dragon."

"He slays the dragon." Gwyn slammed the photos down on the desk. "Oh, that's just great."

"Gwyn."

He heard the warning in Maddie's voice, but the idea that anyone could talk that way about Hermit was too much. Gwyn didn't know how to stop himself. It was like going off the edge of a cliff. "Dragons aren't evil!"

Dr. Mews drew back, but he still looked calm. "You shouldn't contradict your elders, boy. Of course they're evil. It's not just Wagner's idea. Read *Beowulf*. Dragons hoard treasure. They breathe fire and spit poison. They murder innocent people."

"Right. Stupid, six-limbed, bat-winged, drooling monsters with fangs. What chance did they have once people started to think like that? It's Viking nonsense." Gwyn knew he sounded just like Hermit, but it felt good to speak the truth about dragons out loud. Dr. Mews wasn't like other people. Maybe he would listen.

"It's not nonsense! It's tradition. That's what's wrong with young people today. No respect for your elders. You play some computer game or something and suddenly hundreds of years of wisdom mean nothing to you." Now Dr. Mews was shouting.

Maddie placed herself between them. "What if there was an older tradition?" she said in a reasonable tone. "One of befriending dragons?"

Gwyn was breathing hard, but he waited to see what Dr. Mews would say.

The archivist suddenly looked frail and ancient as he gathered the photographs, shoved them into the envelope and handed it to Maddie. "There is no such tradition. Dragons are evil, period. I thought the two of you were different. You gave me hope for the future. Now, I see I was wrong."

"You sure are wrong," Gwyn replied. Part of him wished he could just shut up, but he could not be sorry for defending the dragons.

"Gwyn!" Maddie turned to the old archivist. "Dr. Mews—" she began.

"No one so young has ever used that tone of voice with me. Your brother is no longer welcome here." He waved a shaky hand toward the door. "Just go."

They left quickly because it looked as if the old man might cry, and Gwyn guessed that was something Dr. Mews could never forgive them for seeing. The argument had taken less than a minute, but their friendship was so badly broken, Gwyn wasn't sure it could ever be fixed.

"Well," Maddie said as they reached the street, "that was a disaster."

"What was I supposed to say? Everyone's got the wrong idea about dragons—they aren't even dragons, they're pterosaurs—and they aren't dangerous, they aren't evil. Everyone's got it wrong and we're stuck with it." Gwyn's shoulders sagged.

To his surprise, Maddie agreed. "That's what we are, Gwyn, stuck with it. And you're going to have to learn to control yourself. Dealing with Hermit's going to be hard enough without taking on the world. We're talking about the rest of our lives here."

The weight of this truth crushed Gwyn. "Isn't there any way out?"

Maddie frowned. "Maybe. If a Viking curse really made people forget how dragons were and the weaving tablets can undo it, then we'd better get to those weaving tablets."

Gwyn's mouth fell open. "How?"

Maddie shook her head. "I don't know. We should ask Hermit."

But when they got home their mother called them into the kitchen before they could go upstairs. "The dishwasher was running when I came home. It's almost empty, and there was no soap in it. There's a Mendelssohn CD on the counter covered in scratches. Do you know how any of this is happening?" She looked as if she might cry.

Before Gwyn could say anything, Maddie spoke. "It's the Rae dragon. Gwyn and I found him a few weeks ago. He's been in the house ever since."

Gwyn stared at her. He knew Maddie couldn't lie, but did she have to tell the truth? He waited to see what would happen next.

Annette patted her hand. "Honey, I think it's wonderful that you still play these imaginary games with your brother. Gwyn seems much happier. Are you sure you don't know what's going on?"

Maddie looked bewildered, and Gwyn took the chance to jump in before she could speak again. "We can't explain it, Mom."

"Well, then, I'll just have to hope it goes away."

She looked a little better when they left her, but Maddie bounded up the stairs with angry energy. "Hermit," she said when they found him in Gwyn's room, "you've got to stop playing with the appliances."

The little dragon hung his head. "I just want to see how they work. It's hard to resist. And I didna mean to ruin the music disc. I'm very sorry about that."

Maddie was calmer when she spoke again. "Look, I know this isn't easy for you. It's going to be a lot harder in the summer when Dad's home more. One day, Gwyn and I will have places of our own and you can do what you want, but for now, you're going to have to stick with the computer. Promise?"

"Very well," Hermit agreed, but he did not look happy, and Gwyn understood. It had to be like being under house arrest. An idea popped into his mind.

"Look, leave stuff alone and I'll find a way for us to have some fun," Gwyn promised.

"Anyway, that's not what we wanted to talk to you about," Maddie continued. "Hermit, if this Viking curse is broken, will people know that dragons aren't evil?"

"Madoca always said no one would ever know the

dragons had been friends to mankind until the curse was undone."

"Well, Gwyn and I would like that to happen, we really would, but you have to understand it's going to take time. Maybe I could study something at university that might lead to a job at The Rooms one day."

"Yeah, and that will give you time to learn to weave," Gwyn said.

Maddie gave a short, bitter laugh. "Thanks a lot."

The tiny dragon drew himself up to full height. "I canna tell you how pleased I am to find you've accepted this challenge. I've waited centuries, I'll gladly wait a few decades more. You're young and this is a daunting task, but take heart. When a bit of magic is needed, I've known it to appear."

Magic again, Gwyn thought. If there was any magic to spare in the world, they were going to need it.

o o o

The next day, after they'd eaten lunch, Gwyn got the old hot-air corn popper down from the top cupboard. "What are you doing with that?" Maddie asked.

"We're going to have some fun. Hermit, do dragons ever catch bugs?"

Hermit nodded. "Why do you suppose they call them dragonflies?"

"Oh! Great." Gwyn counted six kernels of popcorn into the popper. He left the plastic top off and plugged it in.

"Gwyn, what are you doing?!" Maddie shouted over the noise. "Those things are going to fly all over the place."

Gwyn smiled. "Exactly."

Hermit caught on and poised himself, hovering just under the high kitchen ceiling. When the first kernel popped, he darted out, flipping it off his wing tip into his open mouth. He spun around to catch the others while Gwyn and Maddie stared, slack-jawed with wonder. Hermit batted the last one into Gwyn's hair.

It became Hermit's favourite game. Gwyn had to listen to his mother complain about stray pieces of popcorn in the kitchen, but she was happy the appliances had started to behave again.

CHAPTER SEVENTEEN

THE HERITAGE FAIR

"Can we see it now?" Annette called from the kitchen.

"Not yet," Gwyn replied. He adjusted the display board holding his Heritage Fair project on the dining room table, trying to see it through the eyes of the strangers who would view it tomorrow. From the centre of the main panel, Daniel almost looked as if he approved. "Okay, you can come in now."

"Oh, Gwyn, it's wonderful!" His mother was gushing, but, to Gwyn's surprise, he found he actually liked it.

He reached out and detached one of the essays. "They come off, see? This is the one on Daniel's ideas about the evolution of flight. It was the hardest to write. You can read it if you want."

Tom took the essay, but he was still looking at the display. "So that's Daniel."

"I think he looks like you, Tom," Annette said.

"I do too," Maddie added.

"What an interesting office," he continued. "Look at all those specimens on his shelves." Then he paused. "What on earth could that be?" He pointed directly at Hermit.

Maddie detached Daniel's biography. "Look, Mom. Here's what Gwyn wrote about Daniel's life."

Gwyn knew Maddie was distracting their mother so she wouldn't notice their dad was pointing at something she couldn't see.

Gwyn took a deep breath. "What does it look like?"

Tom shook his head. "I don't know. A stuffed lizard? Odd, it seems to be smiling."

"Taxidermists must have had a lot of fun in those days," Gwyn replied.

"Well, best of luck with the Heritage Fair tomorrow, Gwyn. I'm sure you'll do well."

Gwyn let himself breathe again. Tom was no longer looking at the image of Hermit.

Annette looked up from the biography of Daniel Rae. "Yes, you've done a great job here. Sunny was telling me the provincial finals for the Heritage Fair are going to be displayed in The Rooms at the same time as her Viking exhibit. Imagine. If Gwyn were to make the provincial finals, both of you might have work on display in The Rooms at the same time."

Maddie shook her head. "My weaving may not make it into the Viking display. The other kids in my textile arts class picked up tablet weaving like they were born to it. I'm still trying to make one band with no mistakes."

"Maddie! Don't look so upset, dear. It's not the end of the world." Annette smiled. "It doesn't matter to me whether either of you has work in The Rooms."

Maddie smiled back, but even Hermit had been discouraged when he'd seen her latest effort. If ending the curse depended on Maddie's weaving skills, they were in trouble.

"So, Gwyn, what happens tomorrow?" Tom asked.

"We're in the gym all afternoon so everyone in the school can see our projects and ask questions, and in the evening anyone can come. That's when they announce the winners."

"We'll be there!" Annette said. "The whole family."

Not quite, Gwyn thought. He and Hermit had argued non-stop about the Heritage Fair for days. He was sorry to be going back up to his bedroom now.

"How did they like it?" Hermit asked as soon as he walked in the door.

"They thought it was great."

"Well it is great, laddie. You've done a marvellous job. If only I could see what people at your school have to say about it—"

"Hermit, let's not go there again. I'm not taking you to school with me. My father noticed you in Daniel's photograph." Gwyn could hear his family moving around outside their bedrooms downstairs. He was having a hard time keeping his voice to a whisper.

"But your father will only be there in the evening," Hermit coaxed.

Gwyn had not forgotten the nightmare he'd had just after they'd found Hermit. It still filled him with dread, and he would never, ever take Hermit to school, but he didn't say any of this. "I'd be too distracted with you there. I need to be able to answer questions. You can't come."

The crest on Hermit's head fell. "If you say so." His voice was low, and his chin brushed the bed.

It was all a bit too studied. Gwyn suspected Hermit was playing him. "Good. I'm glad that's sorted out."

o o o

Over the past two weeks, while he'd finished the project, Gwyn had tried to forget about Dr. Mews. But in the night, he dreamed he could see the parking lot outside his school gym and Dr. Mews was there. Somehow, Gwyn knew that he was inside at the Heritage Fair, answering questions about his project and having a great time.

Dr. Mews was dressed in a black academic gown, the kind Gwyn's father wore for graduation ceremonies at the university from time to time, only this one was in tatters. Dr. Mews paced the icy ground outside the gym door, which was locked. "I canna get in," he cried, rattling the door. "I canna get in." It was Hermit's voice.

Gwyn woke in a cold sweat. The dream shouldn't have scared him, but he was relieved when he saw Hermit was asleep and safe. Gwyn scooped some clothes off the floor and slipped down to the bathroom as quietly as he could, glad that he'd left his project in the dining room.

Before he left for school, he made himself a lunch so he could stay all day. He didn't want to give Hermit another chance to argue.

Students who were in the Heritage Fair had the morning off to help set up the gym. Mr. Banfield, the history teacher, worked from a floor plan he'd made, assigning everyone to collect small tables and chairs from all over the school. Gwyn was relieved to find himself far away from the table-hauling team that got Tyler Cull. Soon the gym was transformed into rows of tables with aisles between.

"Good work, people," Mr. Banfield said. "Time to set up your projects. Before we break for lunch, walk around and see what everyone else has done. You'll be too busy this afternoon to go anywhere. I know you've all worked hard and I won't be surprised if one of you ends up at the national finals in Ottawa."

All morning, Gwyn had wondered what moment in history, what life or event, could possibly have sparked Tyler's interest. Here was his chance to find out. He circled around, pretending to be equally interested in all the projects. Two girls had chosen the Knights of Columbus Hall fire, the World War II tragedy that had taken the lives of almost a hundred people just across the street from the Kirk. Gwyn remembered passing the granite monument the day he and Maddie had found Hermit. There were projects on traditional fiddle music and net making. Bunny's project was about traditional food, and she was getting ready to give out samples of fish cakes and toutins. Gwyn smiled. His mother had never approved of those cakes of fried bread dough. He hadn't tasted one since his Nan died.

So many good projects. Gwyn hadn't really thought about the competition part, but now he really wanted to win, to show everyone Daniel had been a serious person, not just some oddball always talking to himself. When Gwyn was sure Tyler was somewhere else, he rounded that aisle to see his project. And there was a model of Fort Townsend, the beautiful fort, shaped like a star with eight points, now lost forever. Tyler's essay started with the first year of construction in 1779.

"Wow," Gwyn said out loud. It was impressive.

"It's not like I have a fancy relative to write about." Tyler's harsh voice made Gwyn jump. He'd obviously stopped to check out Gwyn's project.

They hadn't spoken since the day Maddie had warned him off. Gwyn turned to face Tyler. He had sounded angry but looked, well, embarrassed. And, Gwyn thought, he's left me alone. Maybe I can budge a little. "So, how did you get interested in Fort Townsend?"

"My nan has an apartment that she rents to students. She used to rent it to one from Quebec who studied archaeology."

Gwyn grinned. St. John's could seem like a small town sometimes. "Angelique?"

Tyler smiled. "Yeah. How'd you know?"

Gwyn explained about birdwatching with her and her boyfriend. "They were both really angry about Fort Townsend. I remember."

Tyler nodded. "Angelique had maps and things and she took me out one time, walking around before they built The Rooms." He pointed to a reproduction of an old sketch showing a view of St. John's Harbour from the ramparts of the fort. "You could still see that platform where the cannons were. It was just a long lump of earth, but Angelique said they could have excavated it. They should have kept that whole field as an archaeological site and built The Rooms farther back."

"I know!" Gwyn said. "They could have done so much with that place. It just kills me." Then he realized Tyler had spoken a complete paragraph without making a threat. For a moment, Gwyn had forgotten who he was.

"Wouldn't it be great to win?" Tyler continued. "I've never been anywhere. It would be my first time on a plane."

Gwyn looked around. People were leaving the gym. Tyler seemed friendly, but Gwyn wasn't going to push his luck. "I guess I'd better be going." As he made his escape, he could have sworn he saw something like regret pass over Tyler's face. Who was this guy, really? He'd never been on a plane. He didn't seem to have parents, and, as far as Gwyn could tell, he'd never had a friend. For the first time, Gwyn wondered how hard it was to be Tyler Cull.

Gwyn bolted a sandwich in the lunchroom, sitting with kids he'd known since kindergarten, sure that Maddie would keep Hermit company at home. When it was time to go back to the gym, Gwyn recognized the fluttery feeling in his stomach from Christmas concerts in early school years—stage fright.

Sitting on a chair beside his project, Gwyn was eager to answer questions about Daniel and his ideas. But the photocopy of the newspaper article about the shipwreck with its headline "TRAGEDY AT SEA" seemed to be the only thing that caught anyone's attention, that and the fact that Gwyn was related to Daniel. When the judges finally appeared, Gwyn could hardly wait to talk to them.

There were two judges, and Gwyn was surprised to find he recognized the woman, who looked like someone's grandmother. They'd never spoken, but he'd seen her at bird counts for years. Her name tag read "Dr. May O'Donnell," and she introduced herself as a retired history professor. The other judge was a man who wrote books about local history. He silently read Gwyn's essays while Dr. O'Donnell asked questions. She smiled when she realized he'd been working in the Mews Annex. "Graduate students have been turned away by Dr. Mews. You're lucky he liked you," she said.

At least she'd used the past tense. Dr. Mews had liked him—once.

"So," she continued, "do you feel your ancestor made a significant contribution to our understanding of the evolution of flight?"

Gwyn shook his head, remembering what his father had said. "No, my project just shows how thinking changed in his lifetime. Before this, everyone thought dinosaur bones had been left by creatures that didn't get onto Noah's ark. In Daniel's time, ordinary people started to understand the science around them. That's why my project is important."

The judges smiled. "Very good!" Dr. O'Donnell said. "You're Tom Rae's son, aren't you?" she added with a note of caution in her voice. "Did he help you with this?"

"He helped me find books and newspaper articles in the university library and we talked about them, but he didn't even see this project until I showed it to my family last night."

The judge who had been reading the essays spoke for the first time. "I must say, you've absorbed the time period. The essays even sound Victorian."

Before Gwyn could think of a reply, Dr. O'Donnell said, "That's what happens when you work with primary source material. The spirit of the times gets right under your skin." Her tone of voice told Gwyn he'd done well.

Was his project good enough to win? Gwyn wondered as the afternoon passed.

He dreaded seeing Hermit when he got home, expecting him to be sulky and resentful, but the little dragon waited on Gwyn's bed, his eyes bright with excitement. "Tell me all about it, lad. I'm dying to hear."

Gwyn recounted everyone's reactions to their project and his response to Dr. O'Donnell's questions. "I do wish I could have seen it," Hermit said finally. There was no bitterness in his voice, just genuine enthusiasm.

Without Hermit's help, Gwyn knew, he wouldn't have made half the effort. He owed the little guy. "Look, you can't come tonight. My dad will be there. But, if I get into the provincial finals, we'll figure out a way to get you into The Rooms so you can have a look."

Hermit launched himself straight into the air, almost hitting Gwyn's ceiling. He hovered for a moment, sending the papers on Gwyn's desk flying to the floor. Even before he landed, Gwyn regretted the promise. Every instinct told him this was a mistake. He avoided Hermit's eyes. "Dad will be home soon and he'll want to know how things went." Gwyn knew, if he stayed, he'd try to talk Hermit out of the idea and they'd argue again. At least now I have a reason to be happy if I don't win, he thought as he went downstairs.

Dinner was a blur for Gwyn. He barely ate and found it hard to sit still while Maddie and his parents asked him about the Heritage Fair. No detail was too trivial to interest them. After months of failing tests and bad grades, Gwyn found himself soaking up the positive attention that only Maddie had been getting lately. He'd come to think of his parents' approval as something that belonged to his childhood, something he'd lost forever. Now, he realized he could have it again—if he put in the grunt work. And he was tired of being bored, of doing nothing, of learning nothing. Maybe it was time to get back to work.

It was such a simple thought, but somehow, it lifted the cloud that had been hanging over Gwyn since last summer. It was as if he'd been lost in the woods for months and suddenly stumbled on the way out, long after he'd given up hope.

"I said, do you want dessert, Gwyn?" His mother's voice seemed to come from far away.

"What? Oh, sorry. No, I'm not really hungry. Jitters," Gwyn managed to reply.

Annette smiled. "Well, after then. We can have a little celebration."

"If I win, you mean," Gwyn replied.

"No, we'll celebrate no matter what happens."

Gwyn smiled. Everyone smiled.

Tom glanced at his watch. "Showtime."

When they arrived at the school, Tom said, "I'm glad we could walk here. Look at that parking lot." It was already full.

Inside, Gwyn and some other kids slipped past the waiting crowd to get into the gym. Tyler was already at his project. He smiled across the aisles, and Gwyn found it easy to smile back. He felt a serious, deep happiness. Nothing so small as losing this contest could take that away from him.

Most parents turned out to be as trivial as their kids. "How are you related to Daniel?" and "Oh, wow, he died in a shipwreck." Gwyn heard the same comments over and over. Finally, it was time to announce the winners.

Gwyn's family had avoided hovering by looking at other projects and chatting with friends, but they came to his side as the judges took the stage. Gwyn saw an old woman in a shapeless winter coat standing with Tyler Cull. She had to be his grandmother.

Mr. Banfield stepped up to the microphone. "Well, this has been our most successful Heritage Fair to date. So many of the projects combine imagination with serious historical research. We're one of the last schools in the area to hold our Heritage Fair. The provincial finals will be a few blocks from here, at The Rooms, in just two weeks. Whoever wins that competition will go on to represent Newfoundland at the national Heritage Fair in Ottawa. We can only send three projects to The Rooms and our judges have had a hard time picking those winners. First, we'd like to present the certificates for honourable mention."

Tom's hand came to rest on Gwyn's shoulder, a solid comfort. Gwyn knew what his father was telling him: don't be disappointed. Gwyn braced himself. Five projects were named and Bunny's was last. Gwyn was sorry. He'd thought she had a good chance of making the finals. But he was still in the running. Either that, he thought, or my project wasn't worth noticing.

Dr. O'Donnell took the microphone. "We won't keep you in suspense any longer. The three winning projects are:

Patricia Dunne and Chantelle Trimm for 'The Knights of Columbus Hall Fire, 1942' . . ." She paused while the two girls squealed and hugged each other. "Tyler Cull for 'Fort Townsend.'" Gwyn looked across the aisles. Tyler's grandmother's face was lit with delight while Tyler smiled at his shoes. Then Dr. O'Donnell spoke again. "And Gwyn Rae for 'Daniel Rae: A Victorian Naturalist Examines the Nature of Flight.' Please come up and receive your certificates."

Gwyn was numb. "Off you go," his mother urged gently, and he found himself walking toward the stage. The clapping continued for a long time after the four finalists took their certificates. When they left the stage, a photographer from the local newspaper took pictures.

"I wish I'd thought to bring our camera," Annette said later as they left the gym. "Honey, we're so proud of you. Not just for winning, for putting in such a good effort."

Gwyn's spirits soared, just as Hermit had that afternoon, but that memory brought him back to earth with a thud. Now, Hermit was going to The Rooms.

CHAPTER EIGHTEEN

THE HOLOCENE MASS EXTINCTION

"I n all my years, I've never seen anyone who's all thumbs the way you are, Maddie."

Maddie looked at her hands in dismay. Hermit was only being honest, Gwyn knew. They were sitting in Maddie's bedroom while Gwyn's parents did the Saturday morning grocery shopping.

"If I don't give Ms. Keats a good weaving this week, I'll be left out of the display. Why am I so bad at this?"

"Dinna be too hard on yourself. In Madoca's time, girls were set to the loom as soon as they could hold a shuttle."

Maddie threw her finished belts onto the bed. The patterns were full of flaws, the edges uneven. "I'm going to give it one more try."

"That's the spirit, lass."

Gwyn heard voices downstairs. "Mom and Dad are back. We'd better go." Hermit clambered onto his shoulders and Gwyn shot upstairs.

"You're sure you've shown me all your lessons for the week?" Hermit asked. For some reason, the word "homework" escaped him.

"We did everything last night." He'd given in to make Hermit happy. Good thing his parents had been out at a party, Gwyn thought. They'd have wondered what was wrong with him.

"Well, that's a pity. I've finished reading your biology textbook. I canna wait to get at it. Do you think you'll get through the whole book this year?"

Gwyn laughed. "We usually don't. Hermit, why are you so interested in learning?"

Hermit looked affronted. "It's my job, laddie! The dragons were like a library."

"What sorts of things did the dragons know?"

"Useful information, about metal-smithing and navigation, but Madoca said they knew other things, too. Bits and pieces. I've been thinking about that since I came here. The things that made no sense must have been very old, maybe some of them were from the days when the stone circles were new." Hermit sighed. "Even if the dragons had survived, no one would need us now." He jerked his head toward the computer. "Books were bad enough. Now, you've got those things."

Gwyn didn't like to see him discouraged. "I bet you know stuff that isn't written down anywhere. Why don't you teach me something?"

Hermit's eyes glinted. "Well, the dragons had another purpose. Once, we connected people to everything around them. By the time the Vikings came, that connection was hanging by a thread but it was still there. When that was broken, the world changed."

"What do you mean?"

"When people listened to us, the dragons were able to hold the world in balance, to keep people from taking too much, from overrunning nature. When the Vikings came to Orkney, they snapped that thread. It was a turning point in history. Mankind went from taking what was needed to taking more and more and more. The world has never been in balance since. And now, it seems wildly out of kilter to me."

The hairs on the back of Gwyn's neck prickled. "A lot of people think exactly the same thing."

"They do?" Hermit nodded. "Maybe that's a sign the curse is weakening."

"How did the dragons keep everything in balance?"

Hermit shook his head. "Och, I haven'a been able to interest anyone in that for centuries. Witchcraft, they called it, then a heathen ritual. I could never make them understand."

"Was it some kind of religion?"

Hermit snorted. "No. The Picts had their gods. This wasn'a part of that. It was probably much older. It's a kind of discipline of the mind. It teaches a way of . . ." He paused, struggling for the right words. "Not a way of looking at the world, that's too shallow, a way of sensing the world, of *being* in the world, that cultivates respect."

"Could you show me?" Gwyn asked.

"You're serious? The lad who willna learn Latin, thank you very much?"

"This sounds more fun than Latin."

Hermit sighed. "It mightn't work, laddie." He glanced toward the stairs that led to Maddie's room. "So far, we've had limited luck with the old skills."

"But we could try anyway, couldn't we?" Gwyn tried to keep his voice calm, barely letting himself hope it might work. It sounded like magic.

"Very well," Hermit grumbled. "I should be pleased. All these years I've waited for someone to show an interest. It seems too late now, though, for it to be any use. Lie down and close your eyes. We're no going about this the right way at all. You should have been trained to look inside yourself first."

"Oh stop complaining. Just try it."

"Listen to me, then. Picture yourself just where you are. Now, I'm going to take you outside yourself, over the city ..."

Hermit's voice didn't exactly disappear. It somehow blended into the picture that formed almost immediately in Gwyn's mind. He was above the house, looking down at his street, his neighbourhood, then, the city with the harbour and Signal Hill, Quidi Vidi Lake just beyond. It was like looking down from a plane. His range of view increased and he could see the far fjords that Newfoundlanders call bays, Conception Bay just over the next land rise and beyond that Trinity Bay. Gwyn pictured all this easily, though it was more vivid than any picture. He zoomed out, effortlessly, until it was like a satellite image. He could see all of Newfoundland, then North America and Europe. Clouds hid most of the planet from view, but somehow he saw it anyway.

Hermit's voice found him again. "Now, you are a part of everything you see. Surrender to that. Let it be."

This was harder. Gwyn felt his mind reach out, probing — for what? As soon as he asked, he felt it. For a few seconds, his whole body tingled as his hand had when he'd held the old manuscript and Daniel's key, then it seared him like a bolt of lightning. He was *everything* on the planet, the rocks, the sea, the soil, the trees and grass that grew from the soil, everything from single-celled bacteria to whales, and all things human, too. The buzz and thrum of life poured like water into every cell of Gwyn's body. It was almost too much to bear, but at the same time, it satisfied a longing Gwyn knew he'd always felt.

Just when he was starting to enjoy himself, he sensed something else, a huge, tsunami-like pulse above it all, a black, throbbing energy that was coming, coming to crush everything in its path. In terror, he withdrew.

Gwyn was back on his bed, gasping like a fish out of water.

Hermit ignored his discomfort. "I must say, you've done remarkably well. It should take ages before even the most adept dragon seer can view the entire planet."

Maybe because I'm used to seeing the planet, Gwyn thought as he struggled to collect himself. Finally, he could speak. "What was that huge thing?"

"You felt it too, did you?" Hermit replied. "Something's wrong. That's what I felt the first day, out in the snowstorm, remember? And again when we went around the lake. It wasn'a just fatigue. What did it seem like to you?"

Gwyn tried to describe it. "Something huge, like a wave, a force—"

"That's what it is, laddie. You've put your finger right on it."

"What?" Gwyn asked.

"Change," Hermit replied. "An enormous change that's building like a huge wave."

"Just change? Hermit, things change all the time."

"This isn'a just change, laddie. You felt the scale of it. What did it seem like?"

"Like the whole planet is about to change, and quickly."

"That's happened before, has it not?" Hermit asked. "I read about it in they books your father brought home about the time when dragons were everywhere."

Gwyn smiled. "Pterosaurs."

"Aye, whatever you want to call us. Things changed and most of us were gone." Hermit nodded toward the computer. "We can find out more in there, can we no?"

"I suppose." Gwyn sat in his desk chair. "Where do we start?"

"Try 'mass extinction.'"

Gwyn laughed. "Mass extinction? The last one of those happened sixty-five million years ago." But as soon as the list came up Gwyn saw something called "Holocene mass extinction" repeated over and over. He opened a page and read for a moment. "Holy cow."

As they surfed from site to site, Gwyn pulled inward, trying to find a way to protect himself from what he was reading.

"You're awfully quiet, laddie," Hermit said when they finally shut down the computer.

Gwyn stood and unclenched his jaw. "I thought I knew about nature. Turns out I knew squat. I've got to ask my dad about this."

"Wait," Hermit began to say. "We need to talk—"

But Gwyn brushed him off. "Later. We'll talk later."

Downstairs, Gwyn found dinner was almost ready. He grabbed a handful of cutlery without waiting to be asked, shoving forks and knives onto the table. If he stopped moving, he felt he might explode. Why hadn't anyone told him about this? Especially his father. He could barely wait until everyone had served themselves before he asked.

"Dad, what do you know about the Holocene mass extinction?" Gwyn asked as soon as they started to eat.

Tom's fork paused in mid air. Gwyn watched him collect his thoughts. "I'm familiar with the concept." He was using his scientist's voice, challenging Gwyn to be rational.

"The concept? Like this is a hypothesis? I spent all afternoon reading about it. We're in the middle of a mass extinction, just like the one that wiped out the dinosaurs."

Maddie stared at him. "What are you talking about?"

Gwyn turned to her. "Plants and animals are disappearing all over the earth. Maybe one hundred times faster than they should be . . ."

"One hundred times faster! That's got to be some kind of mistake."

Gwyn looked at his father again. "You'd better tell her."

"That's the low estimate, Maddie. Some say it's happening one thousand times faster than it should."

"Right," Gwyn continued. "If we're lucky, 20 percent of the world's species are going to disappear, but it could be 50 percent. We're sitting right in the middle of it, and you knew, Dad. Why didn't you tell me?"

"I haven't exactly been hiding this, Gwyn. For hundreds of years, fishermen came from all over Europe to Newfoundland. Why?"

"To fish for cod," Gwyn answered automatically. Part of him was glad his father had switched into teaching mode. They'd been having this kind of conversation all his life and the familiarity of it helped to ground him now.

"That's right. When John Cabot first came here in 1497, the cod were so thick in the water they slowed his boat's progress."

"They let down baskets," Annette said, "and pulled them up full of cod."

Gwyn nodded. Everyone who lived in Newfoundland knew that.

"The moratorium started before you were born, Gwyn, so it's history to you. No one ever imagined we could harm that fishery. But it's ended. Thirteen years. That's how long the moratorium has lasted and the cod stocks aren't recovering. It's worse than that, though. When I was a boy, even when your mother first moved here in the 1980s, you could walk to the end of any wharf and look into the water and you'd see life. Flatfish, sculpins, crab, the ocean was teeming. When you look now, what do you see?"

Maddie spoke this time. She looked pale. "Nothing. You're lucky if you see a starfish or a sea urchin. I remember, when I was little, seeing the caplin run." Her face lit with the memory. "They were like a river of black fish in the ocean. But we don't see that now, do we?"

Tom shook his head. "The caplin don't run like they used to. Something's wrong with the ocean. Not just here, around the world. Even the coral reefs are dying. And similar things are happening on land. The frogs are disappearing. Nobody's hiding this but most people don't even know it's happening."

"But why don't they?" Gwyn asked.

His mother replied. "I think, when most people are faced with a problem that big, they just turn away."

Yes, Gwyn thought, but I'm not most people. I never have been. For the first time in a long time, this seemed like it might be an advantage.

"Look how long it's taken us to even begin to think about global warming," Annette added.

"Did global warming cause this?" Gwyn asked.

Tom shook his head. "There's no simple answer." He gave a bitter laugh. "Not that global warming is simple, but it's bigger than that, Gwyn. Climate change is part of it, but it may be the hole in the ozone layer too, letting in too much ultraviolet light, or it could be all the chemicals we've put into the environment. Then there's habitat loss. That's what's going to finish the great apes and the big cats. The problem is us, really, our need to use up everything. We can't stop behaving like this because we haven't even found a way to think about it yet."

While his father spoke, Gwyn started to tingle just as he had when Hermit had shown him the planet. He'd stumbled on the most horrific puzzle, but it was a wonderful one, too. The world needed him, and he would find answers. He had to, no matter how hard it was, or how long it took.

"Why didn't we ever talk about this before?" he asked.

"I thought it would be wrong. Gwyn, when I was your age, people thought the world might be blown apart by nuclear war. I spent a lot of time worrying about something that didn't happen. You can't really blame me for not laying this all out in front of you, can you? What's the point of putting such an overwhelming problem into the head of a twelve-year-old?" The plea in his voice made Gwyn understand that this could not have been an easy decision.

"But you said it yourself. We need to find ways to think about the problem. I'd like to try."

"He's right, Tom. Over the past few weeks, Gwyn's shown us he's growing up. If he wants to face this, we should help him."

Gwyn was surprised. His mother was usually the protective one.

His father still looked grim, but he nodded. "All right. Let's make this our summer project. If we really pour on the steam, you'll have a good picture of the whole problem by the end of the summer. I expect you to take it seriously, though."

"I'd like that," Gwyn said, remembering how flat and dull the days had seemed without the summer science project last year.

A smile of relief crossed Annette's face. "There. What is it they say about a journey of a thousand miles beginning with a single step?"

"Oh, Mom," Maddie replied. "That's such a cliché."

"Your grandmother had a cliché for that," Tom said. "Even a stopped clock is right twice a day."

"Tom! Are you calling me a stopped clock?"

"Not you, the cliché."

As they laughed and bantered, suddenly just being with his family felt like a precious thing to Gwyn. But his mother was wrong. This wasn't a journey of a thousand miles. It felt more like the journey of a lifetime. At least he wouldn't be alone. Not to begin with.

After supper, Gwyn went upstairs with Maddie, wondering how he could possibly tell her what had happened with Hermit earlier that day and how this had led to his discovery of the Holocene mass extinction. She'd made new cardboard weaving tablets because she'd already worn out the first set. At least she'd learned how to set up a weaving. The new tablets were already threaded through yarn that was strung tight between the bookshelf and the headboard of Maddie's bed. It looked like an exotic musical instrument.

Maddie followed Gwyn's gaze and sighed. "Sometimes in gym class there's a kid who's naturally clumsy. It's like the reverse of talent, you know?" Gwyn nodded as if they were talking about a hypothetical person. They could have been talking about him, but Maddie seemed to have forgotten that.

"When we started badminton, there was this girl who couldn't learn to serve. The teacher ended up putting her to the side and she just dropped the bird and missed it, over and over again. Mrs. Wadden said she'd never seen anything like it. I wondered if the girl was faking — it seemed impossible for anyone to be that bad — but she looked so unhappy I knew she wasn't."

She swept her arm toward the weaving tablets. "That's

me with these things. I am never going to get it right. I make every mistake possible, over and over."

"It can't be that hard."

"You think so? Well, try it. I can't even look at them any more. I think I'll see what Mom's doing."

She fled, and Gwyn picked up the shuttle, which was threaded and ready to go. Everything Jonas had said about weaving came back to him. Gwyn sat on the bed and passed the shuttle through the weaving just enough to make the end neat without pulling. Then he put it down and gave the cards one turn. He picked up the flat stick Jonas had left, slipped it in and brought it down hard, pressing the threads evenly onto the line of weaving. Then, he pulled the shuttle back in the opposite direction, repeating the process.

There was nothing to it. Before Gwyn knew what was happening, the weaving was done. And it was perfect.

CHAPTER NINETEEN

THE VIKING EXHIBIT

Gwyn left Maddie's bedroom, walking upstairs in a daze. How could something so difficult for Maddie be so easy for him?

Hermit was waiting. "We have to talk, laddie. What happened this afternoon is part of everything."

Of course it is, Gwyn thought. How could a planetary mass extinction not be part of everything? But he didn't answer. "Have a look at this," he said instead. He'd cut the weaving away from the threads that had held it in place. Now he laid it on the bed. It was about the size of a bookmark, black and red and turquoise.

"It's perfect," Hermit said. "I knew Maddie had it in her."

"Maddie didn't do this, I did."

Hermit was silent for a moment, then he replied. "It fits with what happened this afternoon, Gwyn. Do you not see? The way you connected with the planet so effortlessly, and now the weaving. You're no just a dragon keeper, laddie, you're a dragon seer, like Madoca."

Gwyn laughed. "That's crazy. I can't be. Maddie's the one with magic powers."

Hermit tilted his head. "What do you mean?"

"She ordered these goons to back off when they were bothering Jonas," Gwyn explained, "and they did. She did the same for me. All these bullies obey her like magic."

Hermit chuckled. "There's nothing magical about that. Maddie has the heart of a warrior. When true bravery shows itself, cowards back away. I've seen that before."

"Maddie's not magic, but you think I am?" How could that be? Gwyn wondered.

"Magic isn'a something a person *is*, Gwyn. People dinna go round with magical powers the way they do in fairy tales. Magic doesn'a do the dishes or shine your shoes. Real magic is a force of its own, like the force of nature. It works as it wants to, not as humans would have it work." He paused for a moment, then continued. "So, you're my weaver. I've waited more than a thousand years for the weaving tablets to appear. You can guess what needs to happen next."

"It's going to be impossible to get anywhere near those weaving tablets." Gwyn picked up the weaving. It felt utterly devoid of magic, like the real world. He clung to that.

Hermit just ground his beak, making that funny scratchy noise. "Do you think my being here is possible? Things are unfolding now as they were meant to, I'm sure of it. Gwyn, you know the force that's building is going to sweep over the world, you saw that with your own eyes."

"That has nothing to do with the weaving tablets."

"But it does," Hermit replied. "The curse was cast to obliterate the memory of the dragons and those who loved them, and, in casting it, the Viking seer broke the ties that held man in the web of life. Mankind was freed to take and take and never give back. You can see where that's led. It's taken a long time but finally, accounts are coming due. Madoca's counter-spell holds the promise that the curse can be undone. It seems people are ready to find their places in the web of life again, and, from what you tell me, they want to. But they need to be freed from the curse before it's too late. It's up to you, Gwyn. Can you walk away from the task?" Hermit's eyes shone. The crest on his head had risen like a battle standard.

Gwyn shook his head. "I've never been brave like Maddie. I have no idea how we're going to pull this off." But just as the crest on Hermit's head began to fall, he added, "You know I've got to try. I'll get Maddie."

When she saw the weaving, Maddie cried, "How did you do that?" She made it sound as if Gwyn had played a trick on her.

"I didn't mean to be good at it."

"Well, you are. It's so much better than anything I've made. This is good enough to be in the display."

"That's what I thought, Maddie. You could give this to your teacher so you could be in the display. Then you'd be at The Rooms when they hold the provincial finals for the Heritage Fair."

"What a good plan," Hermit said. "That way, we can all be at The Rooms together."

Maddie raised an eyebrow. "What's he talking about, Gwyn?"

"I sort of promised Hermit he could have a look if I made it to the finals."

"Sort of!" Hermit snorted. "It was a solemn pledge. You're honour-bound to keep that promise, laddie."

"Right. Honour-bound. So it would be really good to have you there too, in case anything goes wrong."

Maddie handed the weaving back to him. "Jonas already asked if I'd help at the weaving workshop. At least I know how to thread the tablets. So I'll be there anyway. It was a great excuse to skip my last soccer game."

Gwyn smiled.

° ° °

"How does anybody tie these things?" Gwyn grumbled, fumbling with his necktie. Why should he have to get all dressed up for a museum exhibit opening?

"Dinna ask me, laddie," Hermit replied. "Is it no a bit garish? A black silk cravat is what you need with that suit. Whatever happened to the cravat?"

"It probably went extinct," Gwyn said. "Just like this one should." Then he realized what he'd said. "Sorry, I shouldn't joke about extinction. If I'm lucky, I'll find out where the weaving tablets are tonight while we're at the opening of Sunny's exhibit. I just hope they didn't put them in a locked display case."

"But you've no spoken to Maddie about using them yet, have you?"

The necktie slumped around Gwyn's neck. "No. I haven't. How do I explain this to her?"

"I think we should try together," Hermit said.

Gwyn nodded, but he was preoccupied with the idea of finding the weaving tablets. "Maybe. We'll see. I've got to ask Dad for help with this tie."

Gwyn's parents were already dressed. While his father helped him with the necktie, Maddie came out of her bedroom wearing a shiny blue dress and nylons. She even had eye makeup on. Annette went over and hugged her. "You look like a princess," she said, and Gwyn thought she was right.

The Rooms was brightly lit, and lots of people were climbing those huge rock stairs. Inside, at the Viking exhibit, Gwyn almost didn't recognize Sunny. She was wearing her fancy new suit and high heels, she had a new haircut and she'd somehow managed to make her face look different. Annette rushed over to hug her and they started to giggle with a kind of nervous delight that made them seem about Maddie's age. It was embarrassing.

Gwyn looked around for someone to talk to and found Jonas chatting with a woman in a flowing orange dress with sleeves that looked like wings. She wore a clunky necklace and earrings and she looked so strange, Gwyn wondered if she was Norwegian, but as he approached he heard her unmistakable Newfoundland accent.

Jonas smiled when he noticed Gwyn. "Ms. Keats, allow me to introduce Gwyn Rae, who is Maddie's younger brother." He turned to Gwyn. "I am pleased to introduce Ms. Keats, our textile arts teacher." His manners made Gwyn feel as if he were wearing animal skins and carrying a club.

Ms. Keats smiled. "You must be the natural weaver. Maddie told me about you. Maybe you'll take my class when you get to our school."

Gwyn smiled back. He could tell a good teacher in about five seconds. This one was a keeper. "I'd like to. Maddie says your class is fun."

"Are you going to help Jonas and Maddie with the workshop?"

"Oh, Gwyn can't." Maddie's voice came from behind him. "He's going to be too busy with the Heritage Fair. He's in the provincial finals here on Friday."

They all fussed about Gwyn's project making the finals while waiters moved through the crowd with trays of tiny snacks. Ms. Keats asked intelligent questions and Gwyn loaded up a little paper napkin with treats. He was having a great time. When they'd finished talking about the Heritage Fair, Ms. Keats said, "Have you seen the weaving tablets yet? They're just over here." She led them to a display case in the middle of the room. It was glassed in on all sides. Gwyn quickly realized there was no way anyone could get near it without being seen and, of course, it was locked.

"See?" Jonas's voice rose with excitement. "Here are photos of tablet weaving from the Viking Ship Museum in Oslo. I have been there many times." The bands in the photographs were just crumbled grey fragments.

"They look pretty old," Gwyn said.

Jonas nodded. "From the eighth century. They were buried for more than a thousand years."

"The weaving tablets must have been in that bog at L'Anse aux Meadows for just as long," Ms. Keats said. "Just look at them!"

The bog had tanned them a rich tea colour and they were smooth and polished. The wood looked alive. Gwyn did a quick count—twenty. That meant there were more somewhere else.

"Attention, everyone." The voice came from the other side of the room. People stopped talking and the director of the museum introduced Sunny, who looked delighted as she took the lectern.

"This exhibit gives us a chance to showcase some treasures that came to light during our dig in L'Anse aux Meadows last summer. We had assumed most of the important artifacts had already been discovered during previous excavations, but we were wrong. One of our exploratory trenches passed through a bog near the stream that flows through the site. Most of you probably know that archaeologists love bogs because nothing rots in peat. If you drowned in a peat bog, you could be found by archaeologists hundreds of years later, looking more or less the way you did on the day you died, only peat-coloured." The laughter sounded a little uneasy and Sunny rushed on. "We'd recovered wooden artifacts before but nothing like the weaving tablets you see in that central case near the doorway." She pointed and everyone in the room looked at the case. Jonas, Maddie, Ms. Keats and Gwyn drew away in unison, like a flock of birds, to allow a better view.

"You only see half the tablets in this display. They're almost certainly Viking in origin but there's something mysterious about them," she continued. "We can date wooden artifacts using tree rings. Dendrochronology it's called, and it works very well for Viking artifacts, normally. But these tablets don't match the tree-ring patterns for any known time. They are literally off the charts. We don't know what that means, and we may never know. Archaeology is full of unanswered questions." She went on, her eyes glowing. "If those tablets could talk, just imagine the stories they'd tell. Picture a young woman, weaving belts by torchlight long into the night for loved ones going off to battle, brave men armed only with swords and spears . . ." She paused. "Goodness, I'm getting poetic." The laughter was more sincere this time, but Sunny looked dazed. She finished abruptly, saying she hoped everyone would enjoy the exhibit, and went to stand with Gwyn's parents.

"I think I'll talk to Sunny," Gwyn said. Leaving the display case he felt a tug, as if he were tethered to it. It should have been creepy, but it wasn't. There was nothing remotely scary about those tablets. He could have looked at them for hours.

Sunny was still talking about her speech. " . . . no idea where that came from," she concluded as Gwyn approached. "I didn't intend to say anything like that.

Pictures just started popping into my mind." She shook her head as if that could clear it.

Annette patted her hand. "This is such an exciting night. You're just keyed up."

"Have you looked at them yet?" Gwyn asked his parents. He wanted to make sure they'd keep talking about the tablets, to see what he could find out from Sunny. They made their way through the crowd to the display case.

"They look very sturdy for something so old," Tom said.

"The bog helped preserve them, of course," Sunny replied, "but they are remarkably strong. I think they could be used."

Gwyn's heart lurched. "Where are the others?"

"In the office they gave me while this exhibit is on, off the atrium." Sunny hesitated, then said, "I'm not supposed to have them in there at all. They should be in locked storage, but I'm finding it hard to let them go."

"Could we have a look?" Gwyn asked.

"Oh, I'm sure that's not possible," Annette began.

But Sunny grinned like a mischievous kid. "No one will notice if we leave for a minute. Follow me." They slipped though the nearby doorway into the hall that ran like a balcony around the atrium. At the back of the building, Sunny led them to a corridor that Gwyn would not have noticed without her. There were public washrooms and a door. Sunny pulled a key card from her little evening bag. "I've got my coat in here."

Behind the locked door was a hallway filled with offices. Sunny's had no windows.

"Wow, it's dark," Gwyn said as she flipped on the light.

"I know. My office at the university is much nicer but it's been handy to have a workspace here. Well, there they are." There was a grey storage box on her desk. Sunny lifted the lid with care, as if it held something alive. "We used a chemical to replace the water so they wouldn't split and crack as they dried out, but even so, they're in fabulous condition."

The tips of Gwyn's fingers tingled. "Could I touch one?"

Sunny bit her lip. "I really shouldn't, but yes, go ahead. To tell the truth, it's a relief to show them to someone else up close like this. They've really gotten to me." She held out the box.

The weaving tablet fit into Gwyn's hand the way the last piece of a puzzle falls into place. He felt complete. "Wow."

Sunny laughed and gently pried the wooden tablet from his hand. "Easy, boy. I don't know what it is about these things. If you could put it into a pill, you could probably save the world." She looked embarrassed. "Just kidding, of course."

Annette laughed with her, but Gwyn noticed his father hadn't taken his eyes off the tablets in the box. He didn't seem to be listening. Not to the people around him.

"It's lovely to see them up close like this, Sunny," Annette said, "but we'd better get back. People will miss you." Tom shook himself like someone waking from a dream.

So now Gwyn knew where they were. As they left the office, he wondered how he could possibly borrow some, just for a day or two.

CHAPTER TWENTY

⋏ LONG-LOST RELATION

"I still think this is a bad idea, Gwyn," Maddie said.

She wasn't even talking about the worst idea. Gwyn still hadn't found a way to mention that.

Hermit replied before Gwyn could answer. "You canna keep me shut in here forever." Crest flattened, eyes downcast, he was doing his best to look pathetic.

"I did promise, and today's the best day," Gwyn added. "Mum and Dad aren't coming until tomorrow."

"Well, I suppose it's okay." Maddie shook her head, as if to disagree with herself, but Gwyn's shoulders relaxed. They'd argued about taking Hermit to The Rooms for days.

"Aye," Hermit added, "and now I can figure out how we get the weaving tablets."

227

"WHAT?!"

"Anything wrong up there? Shouldn't you two be getting ready for school?" Annette's voice drifted up the stairs.

"We'll be down in a minute," Maddie called. She dropped her voice to a furious whisper. "What's Hermit talking about, Gwyn? We agreed to take our time. You must be crazy."

They argued all the way to school. Gwyn tried to explain everything that had led him to this decision.

"It's urgent, Maddie," Gwyn said just before they parted at her school. "If you'd seen what Hermit showed me, if you'd held one of those tablets and felt what they made me feel, you'd understand. I've got to try to get to them."

"At least wait until tomorrow when I'm there."

Gwyn shook his head. "I can't."

"Oh, Gwyn, I don't want you to get arrested," Maddie said as she left him. She didn't look mad now, only worried.

The idea of getting arrested stuck like a splinter in Gwyn's mind. It was still there when he walked home for lunch. Hermit seemed sure that using the weaving tablets would put everything right, but how? Gwyn wondered. Would the dragons return? He couldn't wrap his mind around that. Would people suddenly stop behaving as if they had two extra planets to use up? That seemed just as unlikely. Gwyn had to admit he had no idea how using those weaving tablets would help anything, but he couldn't stop himself from trying. It felt inevitable, as if fate would keep moving him toward the tablets no matter what.

Ahead, just past Gwyn's street, The Rooms loomed on the big field that had once held Fort Townsend. Winter sunlight strafed the landscape, one shaft hitting the building as he watched. The yellow stone walls, the slanted red roofs, even the dark glass of the atrium glowed, as if a giant hand had pointed down from heaven saying, "HERE." Gwyn shook his head. He couldn't afford to go crazy, not now.

Hermit was waiting in the kitchen. "Could we have tuna for lunch?" he asked even before Gwyn put his backpack down.

"Aren't you nervous at all?"

Hermit ground his beak. "We need to keep up our strength. We've a busy afternoon ahead of us. Now, tell me once more where the tablets are stored."

While he made their sandwiches, Gwyn described the location of Sunny's office yet again. "I don't see how we're going to pull this off," he concluded as he set a plate on the floor for Hermit. "There's a locked door, maybe two."

"Dinna worry. If we're meant to get the tablets today, we will. If not, we've got the rest of your life to find a way."

Gwyn managed to force down half a sandwich, then went to get his folded display poster. After Hermit finished eating, Gwyn tidied the kitchen and put on his winter jacket. "Up you come," he said. As Hermit curled around his neck, Gwyn realized the dragon was trembling. "You're scared?"

"I'm no frightened," Hermit replied. "Just thrilled."

Gwyn still found it hard to believe no one else could see Hermit, but the volunteering mother in the main lobby of The Rooms looked right through the small dragon as she checked Gwyn's name against a list. "You're on the fourth floor, dear. The volunteer at the top of the stairs will direct you." She handed him a name tag, adding, "Oh, and The Rooms has waived the usual admission fees for presenters. Feel free to take in the exhibits when you have time."

"This building is much prettier inside than it is from the street," Hermit said, looking around the atrium as Gwyn climbed the stairs.

"That's what everyone says," Gwyn muttered, but he was smiling because Sunny's office was on the fourth floor. It was a small push in the right direction. Gwyn's smile grew when he found his table. It was beside the wall hiding the corridor that led to Sunny's office. He left his poster lying on the table, took off his coat and patted his shoulder. Hermit climbed up again. "Let's have a look around," Gwyn whispered. He pretended to walk to the washrooms that were along the hall from the door leading to Sunny's office. On impulse, he tried that door. It was not locked now. Gwyn slipped inside.

Sunny had her door propped open and she was sitting at her desk, back to the doorway. Gwyn recognized a stack of student papers. Similar piles of essays had been coming and going in his own house all his life. He was trying to think of an excuse for being there when Sunny turned, as if she'd sensed his presence.

"Oh, Gwyn. Your mother told me you'd be here today." She gestured to the papers. "I'm just trying to catch up on my marking. The exhibit took a lot of my time this semester." While she spoke, Hermit slipped from Gwyn's shoulder to the floor and climbed up a bookcase beside Sunny's desk. Though Hermit was light, the move took Gwyn by surprise and he staggered as the dragon pushed off his leg to the floor. "Goodness, are you okay?" Sunny asked.

"Fine, I just lost my balance," Gwyn replied. Now he had to force himself not to watch Hermit. "How's the exhibit going?"

Sunny looked puzzled. "Fine, I guess. The weaving workshop is happening tomorrow. You'll be here?"

Gwyn nodded. "The Heritage Fair displays will still be up."

There was a long pause as Gwyn waited for Hermit

to come back to him while trying not to look at the metal bookcase where the dragon sat.

"Well, I'd better get back to work," Sunny said.

Gwyn knew he had to go. "Okay, see you later. I'll just be outside," he added. This was aimed at Hermit.

Sunny gave him a puzzled smile and nodded. "Okay."

Gwyn forced himself to leave. As he reached the door that led to the public space, Hermit landed on his shoulder. Gwyn turned down the hall and went into the bathroom. "You shouldn't have done that!" he cried. A stall door swung open. The man gave him a strange look, washed his hands and left without saying a word. Hermit ground his beak.

"Very funny," Gwyn muttered.

"That box on Sunny's desk looks as if I could open it myself," Hermit said.

Gwyn checked to be sure they were alone before he replied. "You'd need to be in there without Sunny. That's not likely."

"Aye, but I'd only need a few moments. We'll just see what happens."

Living so close to The Rooms, Gwyn had arrived early. Kids were still coming into the building after he'd finished setting up his display. "Come on. I'll show you the Viking exhibit."

The weaving tablets looked even more impressive than they had when the room was filled with people. Hermit's claws gripped Gwyn's sweatshirt until they pierced the cloth.

"Hey, watch it," Gwyn whispered.

"I can hardly believe they're finally here," Hermit said. "They're smaller than I imagined. You'd only need eight or so. I'm sure I could carry that many if I had the chance."

Gwyn let Hermit look for a long time, understanding his fascination. Finally, he whispered, "We'd better get back." As they left the hall, Hermit leaned toward the tablets as if he couldn't bear to leave them.

Gwyn set Hermit on the rail of the atrium opposite his table so he could look across the open space and down to other levels. Hermit sat quietly, taking it all in, while Gwyn fussed with his display, adjusting the angle of the boards, stepping back to see how it looked.

"Oh, you're the Rae boy, aren't you?" The voice was behind him. Gwyn turned to find the woman who worked in the archives. He struggled to remember her name. She noticed. "Mildred Noftall," she reminded him. "So, this is what you were working on." She stood and read for a long time. "Why, it's wonderful," she said at last. "It's such a nice coincidence that you've made it to the finals."

"Coincidence?"

"Yes, it's an exciting day for us in the archives. Dr. Mews is a judge! He's done that before, of course, but this is the first time the finals have been held in The Rooms." She glanced around quickly and dropped her voice to a delighted whisper. "Who would have guessed he'd accept? This will be the very first time he's set foot in the door. We're giving him a tour of the archives before the judging starts. Isn't that wonderful?"

Gwyn nodded, dazed. Dr. Mews had told him once. How could he have forgotten? His chances of winning would fly out the door as soon as the old archivist walked in. Mrs. Noftall walked away and he sighed, wishing he'd made himself go back to the Mews Annex and apologize. If Dr. Mews thought dragons were evil, it was hardly his fault. Seeing him now was going to be painful.

Because most kids were still in school, it turned out to be a slow day, not nearly as exciting as the Heritage Fair at his school had been. After a while, Hermit said, "I've got to go see the tablets again, laddie. I'm going back to the exhibit."

"You know the case is locked. Don't try anything funny," Gwyn muttered.

"Dinna worry. You can trust me," Hermit called.

Just after Hermit disappeared into the display room, Gwyn saw the judges coming up the stairs to the fourth floor. He recognized Dr. O'Donnell, the retired history professor, from the Heritage Fair at his school. At least there would be one judge who liked his project. Gwyn didn't know the other man, but both other judges towered over Dr. Mews. He looked like a bit of dandelion fluff that might drift away in a strong breeze, and Gwyn burned with shame to think he'd actually yelled at him.

The judges started on the opposite side of the atrium over by the art gallery. Gwyn could only sit and watch their progress, wishing for some of the dumb questions that had distracted him at the Heritage Fair at his school. Hermit had been gone a long time. Gwyn craned his neck toward the museum display room, wondering if he should go get him. The judges were only a few tables away when Hermit returned, perching on the rail across from Gwyn's table again, well out of the way.

"Good luck, laddie," he called as the trio of judges finally approached. Somehow, the ghost of an echo of his voice rang through the vast shell of The Rooms, causing people to look around. The magic that kept Hermit hidden was as thin and fragile as ancient fabric.

The judge Gwyn didn't recognize was about his father's age, tall and broad like an aging football player. He had the air of someone who is professionally friendly, coming at Gwyn with his hand extended, a big smile pinned to his face. "I'm Bertrand Biddiscombe."

Gwyn knew that name. He had a sudden image of his mother ranting at the newspaper about St. John's city

council and how they would trash their heritage pres-
ervation rules the minute any developer waved money
around. Bertrand Biddiscombe was one of the few she
spared because he had a genuine interest in old buildings.
Remembering this, Gwyn felt his own smile grow more
genuine.

"I believe you've already met our other judges," Mr.
Biddiscombe said while he pumped Gwyn's hand. This
spared Gwyn the embarrassment of having to speak to
Dr. Mews. He found it hard to even look in his direction.

An awkward silence followed until Dr. O'Donnell
said, "Is there anything you'd like to tell us about your
project?"

Gwyn realized he should have launched into an enthu-
siastic spiel. He was off to a bad start. "Oh sure." But
he groped for an opening line. He'd been too preoccupied with the weaving tablets to give the Heritage Fair
much thought. He took a deep breath, darting a glance
at Dr. Mews, who appeared to be absorbed in reading
Gwyn's essay about Daniel's life. That made it easier.
Gwyn spoke about Daniel's interest in flight, his life and
the circumstances of his death, but his heart was not in
it. The presentation sounded dull even to Gwyn's ears.
When he finished, Dr. O'Donnell prompted him again.
"At the Heritage Fair at your school, you said something
about why this is important. Could you say that again?"

"Sure," Gwyn said. "History isn't just important places and famous men, wars and battles. It's also about how ways of thinking change over time." He knew he'd done a better job at his school, but he couldn't remember exactly what he'd said then.

Bertram Biddiscombe spoke. "When we were taking a tour of the archives earlier, Mrs. Noftall mentioned that you'd used its resources. Did you learn anything special while you worked there?"

Gwyn nodded. "Dr. Mews made space for my sister and me in his part of the archives. Because of that research, I discovered things I'll remember for the rest of my life." He hoped Dr. Mews might take this as a kind of apology.

"Just doing my job," the old archivist growled. Neither of them looked at the other.

Dr. O'Donnell looked bewildered. "Yes, well, thank you for your presentation."

They left Gwyn with the flat taste of failure in his mouth. That had not gone well. Winning the Heritage Fair was nothing compared to getting those weaving tablets, but at this point both seemed beyond his reach.

Because he was on the top floor, the judges only had to visit a few more tables after Gwyn's. Then they disappeared. They were gone for a long time, until finally a parent volunteer called, "The judges are ready to announce the winners on the second level."

"Stay here on the railing," Gwyn whispered as he passed Hermit. "You'll be able to see everything." He walked around and stood on the stairs where all the presenters from his floor had gathered. The stairs that climbed through the atrium had been made with generous landings where displays could be mounted. From up here, Gwyn had a good view of the entire space. He hadn't seen Tyler Cull all day, but he noticed him now, on the third floor, standing almost under the rail where Hermit was perched. Tyler smiled when their eyes met and Gwyn knew his presentation must have gone well.

"Attention, everyone, please." Bertram Biddiscombe's speech-making voice boomed through the atrium. "We've seen many wonderful presentations here today. Only three will go on to Ottawa for the national finals, but you can all be proud of yourselves. We had some heated debates while picking the winners. After the judging is over, please stay for a while and admire everyone else's displays. Now, Dr. O'Donnell will give you the news you've all been waiting for."

"The winners are: Ashleigh Tilley for 'A History of Boat Making in The Battery,' Lucy Tuong for her project 'An Oral History of the Vietnamese Boat People in St. John's' and, for 'Fort Townsend,' Tyler Cull." Cheers and squeals of surprise went up here and there and everyone clapped.

Tyler looked stunned as he walked down to join the other winners, and Gwyn found himself smiling. Tyler would get his trip to Ottawa, go on his first plane ride. It would mean so much more to him than it would have meant to Gwyn. So that was okay.

Back at his display, Gwyn found he couldn't move from his place near Sunny's office. He just sat there, letting defeat seep into his bones. Losing the competition was not what bothered him. If he'd at least been able to make peace with Dr. Mews, the day would not have seemed like such a complete loss.

Hermit sensed his mood. With one beat of his wings, he left his perch on the railing and curled around Gwyn's neck.

When Gwyn saw Tyler Cull approaching, he forced himself to stand and smile so no one could mistake him for a poor loser. People kept stopping Tyler to shake his hand and congratulate him, so he was almost beside Gwyn's table before the crowd parted. He looked at Gwyn and took a step back, suddenly turning pale. "What the hell is that?"

"Dinna be afeared, laddie," Hermit said.

Gwyn froze. Hermit was talking to Tyler Cull?

"What is that?" Tyler's voice rose as he repeated the question. People were turning to stare. "What are you trying to do to me, Rae?" He looked around, wild-eyed.

"He's got some kind of iguana, right there on his shoulder. It spoke to me. He's got a talking iguana!"

A man stepped forward and put his hand on Tyler's shoulder. "Easy, son."

People crowded around, and Hermit launched off Gwyn's shoulder, gliding to safety in the open air of the atrium where he hovered, effortlessly.

Tyler's bewildered eyes followed, then he fainted.

For Gwyn, the idea of fainting had always conjured the words "graceful" and "swoon," but Tyler dropped like a stone. If the man who was standing with him hadn't caught his shoulder, he would have cracked his head on the floor. This man eased Tyler down and looked up at Gwyn. "Call 911," he said. "We need an ambulance."

Gwyn was halfway to Sunny's office before he realized where he was going. The part of this brain that knew Tyler was going to be okay didn't seem to be talking to his legs. "Phone," he gasped, lunging for Sunny's desk. She gave a startled yelp as she swung her office chair out of his way but grew calmer as she heard Gwyn explain the situation to the 911 operator.

"The fire station is half a block away," she said when Gwyn hung up. "They'll be here in no time. Let's go see what's happening." She left without looking back.

Gwyn did not allow himself to hesitate or think. He filled his pockets with weaving tablets and replaced the lid on the box, leaving Sunny's desk undisturbed. The wooden tablets made bulges in his pockets, but when he pulled his sweatshirt down they disappeared.

Hermit was still hovering in the open space of the atrium and Tyler was lying on the floor, pale and unconscious. What would happen if he woke before the paramedics took him away? Gwyn couldn't let him see Hermit again. He moved to the railing to signal Hermit to come to him, but before he could, Hermit flew over the crowd and paused right above Tyler, the breeze from his wings causing nearby displays to fall over. "Did someone open a door?" Gwyn heard a woman ask. If Tyler opened his eyes, Hermit would be the first thing he'd see. It seemed so cruel, Gwyn shouted before he knew what he was doing, "Herm—" He had to fake a choking fit when people turned, but Hermit came and settled on Gwyn's shoulder. Now, if Tyler should wake, he would only see the crowd around him.

"Did you get the weaving tablets, laddie?" Hermit asked.

Gwyn nodded, one short bob, wishing this could have happened some other way. Tyler came around as the paramedics loaded him onto a stretcher, but he seemed too woozy to focus on anything as he was wheeled to the nearby elevator.

I'll have to find a way to make this up to him, Gwyn thought. But a glow of comfort from the weaving tablets in his pockets made him believe everything was going to be fine.

CHAPTER TWENTY-ONE

THE TABLET-
WEAVING THIEF

"I can't believe you did this!" Maddie cried. The weaving tablets were laid out on Gwyn's bed. There were twelve. "What's Sunny going to say?"

Gwyn hadn't even told her about Tyler Cull.

"Maddie, if I use them tonight and find a way to get them back tomorrow, maybe Sunny will never know." That was his best-case scenario, not the most likely one. Gwyn took a deep breath and plunged on. "I don't know how to set them up and I don't have any wool. I need your help. Please?" He was prepared to get down on his knees and beg if he had to.

"All right." The words rushed out with an angry sigh. "If it gets the tablets back where they belong, I'll help you. Just one weaving, though. You're lucky Mom and Dad went to a movie. Imagine the trouble you'll be in if they find out."

"Bring all your wool, Maddie, please," Hermit said. "Gwyn will know the colours when he sees them."

Gwyn had expected Hermit to be wildly excited, but he'd turned grave since the tablets had come into their possession, as if something terrible was about to happen. The thought of something terrible reminded Gwyn of Tyler. Where would he be now? In hospital? Gwyn only hoped he wasn't in a psychiatric ward. Then Gwyn remembered the question he'd been meaning to ask since they left The Rooms.

"Hermit, why could Tyler see you?"

"There's only one answer for that—he's a child of Madoca, just as you are."

"We're related? Huh. There's not much resemblance."

Hermit nodded. "Twelve centuries is a long time. Madoca had seven children. By the time she died, three were already gone away. Tyler's ancestors might have come from anywhere in Britain, but if you could trace them back, you'd find one from just outside Aberdeen."

Gwyn shook his head. Though he believed Hermit, it would take time to get used to the idea. "I wish he hadn't seen you like that. People are going to think he's crazy."

"Dinna worry about that. I've a bit of magic left in me yet," Hermit replied. "Tyler will remember nothing, and everyone will think he was just a wee bit overwrought, excitement of winning and all."

"That's why you flew above him? I thought you were being mean."

"No, laddie. I was sometimes mischievous but never mean."

It was odd to hear Hermit talk about himself in the past tense, but before Gwyn could ask why, Maddie returned with a paper shopping bag full of wool. She heaped the skeins onto Gwyn's bed.

"These ones," he said without hesitation. He chose creamy white, forest green and ocean blue.

Maddie nodded. "Nice colours. But how about the pattern?" she asked Hermit. "Jonas gave me copies of the pattern charts we're going to use tomorrow. Should I get one?"

"No," Hermit said. "Just take one of the tablets in your hand. You'll know what to do next."

Maddie stood very still when she held the tablet. "Wow," she said after a long moment, her voice hushed. She found the scissors she kept in the bag with the wool and set to work in a kind of trance, with no pause, no hesitation. When she finished, the threaded tablets were strung out between the handle of the wardrobe and the back of Gwyn's desk chair. Maddie shook her head. "That should have been a lot harder. It was almost as if the yarn knew what it was doing."

"What now?" Gwyn asked.

"I'll wind you a shuttle. Which colour?"

Gwyn's hand went for the blue as if it had called to him. He gave it to Maddie. "Are you going to stay in case I need help?" he asked as she snipped the yarn.

She shook her head as she quickly wound the shuttle. "You aren't going to need help, and I don't think I should watch."

"That's right, lass," Hermit said.

She gave Gwyn the shuttle then suddenly leaned over to kiss his cheek. Gwyn couldn't recall the last time she'd kissed him. Then she smiled. "Dinna be afeared, laddie." She caught Hermit's accent exactly, then in her own voice added, "You'll be fine."

After she left, Hermit scrambled up to his lair. "I'll watch from here, Gwyn. Time to start."

Gwyn straddled the chair to face the long strands of yarn tied to its back. His hand trembled when he took up the shuttle, but, as he began to weave, a vast and perfect calm settled on him. It was the way he'd always imagined it would feel to be a field nestled under a blanket of new snow, safe from the killing cold of winter.

Although he always remembered what happened next,

Gwyn could never really summon that feeling again. He turned the tablets, but they moved as they wished, rarely in unison. Sometimes, he was surprised to find they even flipped so that the warp threads changed places. Time seemed to shimmer like waves of heat rising on a summer day, expanding, until Gwyn felt as if he had been with the tablets for all those lost centuries while the weaving grew, tight and perfect, each new line falling into place as if it had to be.

Soon Gwyn realized he was weaving a thin, elongated map of the world, starting with the tip of South America up to the North Pole. Then the pattern wove down the other side of the globe, a squash of Europe and Asia together, to Japan and Australia. While he worked, he felt an overwhelming tenderness for the planet he had always taken for granted, the one place in a hostile universe where life was welcome. As Antarctica emerged, Gwyn knew the weaving was ending. He didn't want to let the planet go, wishing he could hold it forever.

Gwyn came back to himself with the sensation of falling from a great height. He wanted to cry with longing for the place he had just lost. He had to look around, to remind himself he was here, on earth, at home. Gwyn tried to stand, but a heavy hand seemed to pin him to his chair.

"Did gravity just get stronger?" he muttered.

"You're tired, laddie," Hermit murmured. "And little wonder. You've just carried the weight of the world."

Gwyn managed to stagger a few steps to his bed before he fell. "It felt good." He wasn't sure whether he'd spoken the words or just thought them. As he closed his eyes, sleep rushed to claim him like a black tunnel.

o o o

The sun was strong enough to warm Gwyn as he opened his eyes. It was not an early sun. He glanced at his clock. Noon! He had no idea how long he'd slept. He thought at first he must have dreamed everything that had happened, from the moment Tyler Cull fainted on, but the weaving was just where he'd left it. He leaned forward on the bed for a better look. A distorted map of the world should have looked odd and ugly, but it was beautiful. Had it done anything? Would the world change? The tip of Hermit's tail was just visible over the top of the wardrobe and Gwyn did not disturb the dragon as he slipped into his clothes and flew downstairs. It was a new day in a new world. He had to find out what was going to happen.

His mother and father sat at the kitchen table, finishing lunch. "Where's Maddie?" he asked as he poured himself a glass of juice.

"At The Rooms, remember? Helping Jonas with that weaving workshop?" Annette replied. "I thought you were going too, but Maddie said we should let you sleep. You have to be at The Rooms at one for the public viewing of the Heritage Fair projects, don't you? I was just coming up to wake you."

The juice jug wobbled in Gwyn's hand on its way back into the fridge. The stolen weaving tablets would be the first thing anyone would notice if they walked into his room. He took a deep breath. "I still have plenty of time to get over there. Are you coming?"

"Yes, of course," Annette said. "How often will I see both my children in events at The Rooms on the same day?" As Gwyn sat at the table, his mother put her hand on his arm. "You know we're very proud of you, dear. Winning didn't matter. Now, I've got to check the laundry."

Gwyn smiled. She could be proud of him if she wanted.

His father was reading the Saturday paper, not the local paper, the national one. "Anything new?" Gwyn asked, trying to keep his voice casual.

"Same old same old," Tom replied.

Gwyn was glad his father's nose was buried in the paper. He couldn't hide his disappointment. Hadn't he just changed everything? Shouldn't there be dragons over Scotland? Seas full of fish? He'd ask Hermit later.

Now, he had to get to those tablets before anyone saw them. He bolted his toast and rushed back upstairs.

Gwyn found Maddie's scissors, pushed the chair forward to relax the tension on the yarn and cut the tablets out one by one so he could slip each from the web of weaving without dropping them. Their magic spread through the tips of Gwyn's fingers until a warm glow filled his whole body. He wondered if he might keep one, just one little tablet. Who would notice? It seemed the worst kind of wrong for them to be locked away. He took one of the tablets and opened his desk drawer, but before he could slip it in there was a subtle shift in the world. For an instant, Gwyn saw himself to be a single link in a long chain of people touched by the magic of these tablets. The chain stretched into the future as well as the past, and he realized the tablets must stay together. No one could ever really own them. But he smiled as he put the single tablet back with the others, because he was sure they would not stay in The Rooms forever.

Now, though, it was his job to make sure they were all together again. At least today he wouldn't have to worry about Hermit. He glanced to the top of the wardrobe, but the dragon still hadn't stirred.

"Time to go, Gwyn," his mother called.

When they stepped outside, sunshine beamed from a blue sky and streams of meltwater trickled down the street. Patches of grass had appeared and the scent of earth filled the air. Gwyn sniffed as if it were perfume.

"Ah, spring," Tom said. "Weeks of rain, drizzle and fog to follow, but at least we can enjoy the weather today."

"We're not planning to stay long," Annette said as they turned toward The Rooms. "I know you're both too old to want your parents hanging around."

"I don't mind," Gwyn said, and he meant it.

"Well, that's sweet of you, dear, but I don't want to embarrass Maddie either."

Inside The Rooms, Gwyn left his parents while they asked for directions to the tablet-weaving workshop and climbed to the fourth floor where his project sat waiting for him. He slipped around the corner to try the door leading to Sunny's office. It was locked.

Gwyn had barely sat down when Tyler approached, wearing a big badge with "PROVINCIAL WINNER" emblazoned on it. "Are you okay?" Gwyn asked.

"Yeah. The doctors said I was probably overexcited by winning. They said that sometimes does funny things to a person's blood pressure. The strange thing is that I can't remember anything. I was walking toward your table just about here." Tyler shook his head. "The next thing I knew, I was on a stretcher." He looked around as if he might find his memory waiting for him in the atrium. "I wanted to ask you, did anything funny happen?"

"Funny?"

"I have this memory of being really scared but I don't know why."

"There was nothing to be scared of," Gwyn replied. "I'm sure."

"Okay. That makes me feel better. Hey, Rae, I'm sorry you didn't win too."

"That's okay," Gwyn said. "I've already seen Ottawa."

Tyler didn't move. "Yeah, well, I'm sorry I've given you such a hard time. You're not a bad guy."

"Neither are you." Gwyn wasn't sure he was ready to embrace Tyler as a long-lost relative, but the thought that he wouldn't be bullied any more made him smile. "People are probably hanging around your project, you know, waiting for you to show up."

"I guess. I left my nan down there. She knows as much about it as I do. I just had to ask you about yesterday first, to see if I could get it straight in my mind. See you."

As Tyler walked down the stairs, people stopped to shake his hand. Some of them drifted from project to project, asking familiar questions when they reached Gwyn. Between visitors, he wondered if he should leave the tablets somewhere so they could be found, but it seemed disrespectful to just abandon them, and cowardly too. He was still arguing with himself when his parents came to say hello.

His mother studied his face before they left. "You're not still bothered about losing, are you? You look upset."

"No, I'm good," Gwyn assured her.

A few moments later, the elevator along the hall opened and Sunny got out. The floor beneath Gwyn seemed to fall away, leaving him with nothing to hold on to. He'd hoped the missing tablets might have escaped her notice, but he could tell from Sunny's face she knew they were gone. He stood up.

She gave him a searching look, then said, "Do you have something to tell me?"

Gwyn nodded. "Could we go to your office?"

In her office, he took the tablets out of both pockets, carefully, placing them on her desk.

Sunny gave a short cry that managed to sound relieved and annoyed at the same time. "I was only going to wait a few more hours before I called the police. I figured it had to be someone I knew, you or somebody who works here. Do you have any idea the kind of fuss this would have caused if I'd gone public?"

Gwyn winced. "I'm sorry. I just couldn't resist. But I was always going to bring them back. It wasn't stealing really, more like borrowing."

"I understand how they make you feel, Gwyn. When I first found them, I was tempted to keep one or two for myself, but they don't belong to us."

"Are you going to tell Mom?"

Sunny's mouth twisted as if she'd tasted something bitter, then she shook her head. "I promised myself last night, around 3:00 a.m., actually, if they came back safely I'd say nothing to anyone. It was my fault too, keeping them out when they should have been locked away. It was so unprofessional. So this is our secret. Deal?"

"Deal." Gwyn wasn't sure how his legs were holding him up.

Sunny smiled. "You'd better get back out there."

Gwyn gave the tablets one last, longing look before he turned away.

He practically bounced to the stairs. He'd done it. He'd used the weaving tablets to do what Hermit had wanted and now they were back where they belonged. He was glad he hadn't just left them lying somewhere. Sunny had a right to know where they'd been. He and Maddie would still have Hermit to worry about for the rest of their lives, but they would manage. The little guy was part of his life now. Today, though, he was free. Now, Gwyn wanted to see what Maddie and Jonas were doing.

CHAPTER TWENTY-TWO

THE WEAVING WORKSHOP

As Gwyn came down the stairs, he saw a pack of teenagers leaving the lobby below. They were a strange-looking bunch, all laughing and joking. Some were dressed like goths, others wore bright, hand-knit sweaters. Gwyn saw short skirts, long skirts, baggy jeans and ripped tights. One goth girl had shiny purple hair, and that triggered a memory, something Maddie had said.

When he came into the workshop area Maddie looked up from her yarn and smiled. "Hey, you just missed the kids from our textile arts class." She waved her arm around the room. "They thought this was way cool. Jonas and I are going to catch up with them later at Hava Java."

Across the room, where he was teaching, Jonas looked up and smiled at Gwyn.

"It's pretty lonely upstairs today," Gwyn said. "I thought I'd hang out here for a while."

"Everything okay?" Maddie asked.

"Great." Gwyn wished he could shout the word.

"Okay!" Her smile told him she understood. She handed him a pair of scissors. "It's time you learned how to set up a weaving. Cut eight strands of all these yarns into four-metre lengths and we'll take it from there." Maddie worked with a happy energy that Gwyn hadn't seen in a long time. She looked, he realized, like the old Maddie, the one with friends.

The workshop was held in a kind of alcove where the inside wall could be folded back to reveal an open space. It was filled with tiny chairs and tables and looked as if art classes might be held there during school visits. The outside wall was a huge sheet of glass, floor to ceiling, so daylight flooded the room. The tablet-weaving workshop was busy. Gwyn recognized Bunny from his class, but the four other kids with Jonas were all younger, and so was the girl who was waiting for Maddie to get her started.

Gwyn looked at the belts the kids were making. They were terrible, worse than Maddie's, but these kids all had big smiles on their faces. They didn't care.

As he measured and cut the yarn, Gwyn began to wonder all sorts of things. Would weaving still come as easily to him now? If he'd really undone that curse, when would the world start to change? St. John's looked pretty in the sunshine through the huge glass wall, but it seemed the same as always.

When he'd finished cutting the yarn, Maddie showed him how to thread the tablets using one of the pattern charts Jonas had given her, and they set up a thin band of tablet weaving for the girl who was waiting.

Sunny came down from her office and handed Maddie two envelopes. "Here are your cheques." She studied the display of tablet-woven bands made by Maddie's class. "These are fabulous. Do you have one in here?"

Maddie pointed to a band of fine black and fuzzy white wool woven with a tight pattern of concentric squares down the middle. "That's the one Jonas made, but no matter how hard I tried, I couldn't weave one without mistakes. Gwyn's much better at this than I am."

"Oh, he is, is he?" Sunny replied.

Gwyn stared at the wool on the table in front of him, waiting to see what Sunny would say next, but she just glanced at her watch. "You've done a great job here. If no one else shows up you can pack up soon—"

An uproar filled the atrium, as if a pack of wild animals were rushing up the stairs. A group of girls swept into the workshop space—Maddie's soccer team. They fell silent when they saw Sunny, as if they hadn't expected to find an adult.

"Are you girls here for the tablet-weaving workshop?" Sunny asked. "It's a bit late."

Jasmine O'Connor answered her. "We had a soccer game. We were really hoping we might be able to take part in this wonderful event."

Her voice dripped sarcasm, but that wasn't something Sunny would hear. "Well, I suppose we can keep the workshop going awhile longer." She turned to Maddie, also missing the distress on her face. "It'll be nice for you to work with people your own age, after all. Now, I'd like to get home before dark. Just let the front desk know when you're finished and someone will lock up."

Gwyn hated to see Sunny go. "Nice" was not likely to describe what was about to happen.

The girls fanned out as if they owned the place. Jasmine pointed to the bands Maddie's class had made. "I want to make one just like that."

"Jonas made that one," Maddie replied.

Jasmine rolled her eyes in his direction. "Oh, the fashion queen." The other girl giggled as if she'd said something original and witty.

Gwyn watched Jonas, who was helping Bunny. He seemed not to react, but his hand hovered over her weaving a moment longer than it should have. Then he recovered himself and said, "Bunny, don't pull too hard. Leave a bit of slack as you start the next line."

"Bunny! How *cute*!" Jasmine cried. "I suppose your sisters are Flopsy and Mopsy?"

Jasmine's friends laughed as Bunny lowered her head. Gwyn had never seen anyone tease Bunny like this, and she was defenceless. Anger lit a fire under him. Okay, he thought, let's give them something to do. He sorted through the stack of patterns, finding the one Jasmine had liked. He knew enough about weaving to understand it would not be easy. Good.

"Come over here and I'll show you how to set up," he said. They hadn't made the little kids do anything but weave. He fanned the remaining patterns out on the table. "The rest of you can pick patterns."

Faced with actually sitting down and learning to weave, the other girls began to make excuses — it was getting late, they'd only come to see what was going on. By twos and threes they drifted away and Gwyn's spirits rose. Jasmine's kind of meanness required cheerleaders. Without an audience, she'd be neutralized. But she knew that too.

"Wait a minute. Rochelle, Sandy and Moira," Jasmine called. "You were so *interested* in this project. What happened?" She put enough menace into her voice to make the three girls freeze, turn and come back to the table where Gwyn stood with the patterns. Like zombies. It made his skin crawl. He just bet Jasmine's "project" was not learning to weave.

While the three girls picked their patterns, Gwyn said, "Maddie, why don't you tell them how tablet weaving works?" If they could only keep these girls busy, they might not have time to make trouble.

Maddie's voice wavered as she spoke. Where was the fearless warrior who chased bullies away? How could she make herself such an easy target? Gwyn realized he'd probably acted exactly the same way around Tyler. Then he remembered something Hermit had said, "When true bravery shows itself, cowards back away." Gwyn knew he could face this girl down for Maddie. It wasn't his battle, and somehow that made him fearless. Even if Jasmine turned on him, she wasn't going to beat him to a pulp.

Most of the younger kids were finished now. Before Maddie stopped talking about tablet weaving, a few parents arrived to take them home. In the presence of adults, Jasmine kept her cat claws hidden, so that was good. Gwyn and Maddie got the four teenage girls set up to weave before the families left. Only two younger kids remained, the girl Gwyn had helped and Bunny, who sat with her finished belt in her hand, watching.

Now, the focus turned to Jonas. He gave the four girls a hesitant smile as he began and Gwyn's heart sank. If Jonas had been cold and distant, he might have had a chance. Instead, he was inviting these girls to make some kind of connection with him. Gwyn could guess what Jasmine would do with that invitation.

"So," Jonas began, "Maddie has already told you about tablet weaving and now you will learn. May I see the patterns?" he asked Maddie, and she brought them to him. Jonas frowned. "One of you has chosen a difficult pattern. I didn't realize I'd put it in with the others." He gestured to Jasmine's friends. "You all have patterns that will allow you to keep turning the tablets in one direction. But you, what is your name?"

"Jasmine."

"You will need extra help because the tablets must go four turns forward and four turns back. I will show the others how to weave before you begin."

After they'd woven a few lines, Jasmine's friends began to enjoy themselves. "Look at this! It's really pretty," Rochelle said.

"This is fun," Sandy agreed.

All three were catching on quickly and Gwyn thought their belts looked great. But as they wove, Jasmine's face darkened. Her audience was not supposed to enjoy working with Jonas. By the time he turned to her, she looked like a thundercloud. When Jonas asked, "Do you have your shuttle?" her hand flew up as if she was going to punch him. Unlike Maddie, he was not fazed. Gwyn had to admire that. "Very well then, this is a shed." Jonas put a finger between the open threads. "Pass the shuttle through."

Jasmine pulled the shuttle tight, so her weaving bunched in. She had to count the number of times she turned the tablets to make the pattern work, but as soon as Jonas left her on her own she lost track and the weaving looked nothing like it should. This threw her off her game and she seemed to forget why she was there. Good, thought Gwyn, soon it would be time to leave. Maybe they could get through this without bloodshed.

Or maybe not. Jonas noticed Jasmine was having trouble and he was too kind to let her flounder. He reached for her weaving to help. "You see, you must turn back at this point, like so . . . ." He accidentally brushed Jasmine's hand.

She pulled back as if he had burned her. "Don't touch me, you faggot!"

Bunny gasped. Gwyn guessed it was not the word that shocked her as much as the hate in Jasmine's voice.

"Bunny, time to go. Dad's waiting in the car." Everyone turned to a tall teenage boy. From the tone of his voice, Gwyn could tell he'd seen everything.

"Oh, Eric, hi. This is your sister?" Jasmine tried to sound pert, but she'd turned a sickly shade of green.

Eric gave a sharp nod. Bunny rushed to her brother, pushing her weaving into his hand. "See what I did?

Jonas taught me. This is Viking weaving. He's from Norway."

"Hey, Bunny, that's great." Eric smiled at Jonas. "You're Norwegian? Our great-grandfather came from Sweden. He got off a ship in St. John's Harbour and never got back on." He studied Bunny's weaving. "The Vikings did this? Cool." Gwyn had a good view of Eric's face from where he was standing and he saw the other boy's eyes slide in Jasmine's direction for a split second before he spoke again. "They play hockey in Norway, don't they? Do you play, Jonas?"

Jonas smiled. "I brought my skates with me but I haven't played since we came to Canada."

"A bunch of us have a pickup game on Sundays. You'll have to chip in for the ice time but you're welcome to join us."

Jonas smiled. "I would like this very much."

"Wasn't this workshop supposed to be over at four?" Eric said. "I'm sure my dad would like to meet you. He's always talking about taking us to Scandinavia some day. Why don't you pack up and come down to say hi? I'll wait." Eric settled himself on one of the little tables.

"You guys have a lot in common, Eric," Maddie said. "We're going to catch up with some kids from our textile arts class at Hava Java. Why don't you come too?" Maddie didn't look at Jasmine, but her voice wasn't shaky now.

Gwyn smiled. "The rest of you can take your work home and finish it there," he said. "See?" He detached Jasmine's weaving from a hook and let it fall into her lap. It was terrible anyway. "We're finished."

o o o

"Well, Eric sounds fearless. Most boys his age would be afraid that Jasmine would start rumours about them, too," Annette said at supper that night when Maddie finished the story.

"Oh, Jasmine can't hurt Eric," Maddie replied. "He's super popular. With him as a friend, Jonas will be safe. The other kids were stunned when we showed up at Hava Java with him, but they started talking about music and Eric fit right in."

"I'm glad things turned out so well," Annette said.

And she doesn't know the half of it, Gwyn thought. He put his napkin on his plate with a big, contented sigh.

"Maddie," Annette continued, "I got a Jane Austen movie for tonight, *Emma*."

"Terrific," Maddie replied.

Tom began to collect the dishes. "That's odd. I thought they'd wait until tomorrow, but suddenly I hear all those term papers in my study calling, *Mark us! Mark us!*"

Annette laughed. "Why are men so strange about

Jane Austen? *Emma* is quite funny." She gave Gwyn a quizzical look. "I suppose you're busy?"

"I volunteer to fill the dishwasher and tidy up the kitchen."

His mother shook her head. "We can't argue with that, Maddie. Let's go."

Tom stacked the dishes on the counter and disappeared into his office, leaving Gwyn to do the rest. Happiness carried him through the unenjoyable work of washing pots and stacking the dishwasher. Everything about the day had worked out so well. When he was finished, he grabbed a plate of lasagna and some salad, and slipped up to Hermit.

The little dragon had shared Gwyn's joy earlier, but now he was not himself. He said nothing while he ate, and when he sank to the bed his plate was still half full.

"Hermit, what's wrong? You look terrible."

Hermit gave him a long, serious look before he spoke. "I've started to grow."

If he grew, he would age, Gwyn realized.

"Oh, Hermit. How did that happen?"

"The counter-spell's no longer needed, now that the curse is gone."

"Are you going to be all right?"

"In a manner of speaking, laddie. At least, I'm going to be released."

"Released? The magic that's been keeping you young is gone, isn't it?" Nothing as old as Hermit could live. A tear hit Gwyn's hand before he even knew he was crying. He brushed his eyes. "This is terrible."

Hermit climbed into his lap. It was the first time he'd done anything like that. "Is it? I dinna think so. Imagine yourself living so long that everyone you know and love is dead and gone, Gwyn. Now imagine that happening over and over and over again. And every time you met someone, you'd know you'd see them dead one day. It hasn'a been easy, and not just for me. So many times, I'd have to watch a dragon keeper sit and cry because I was keeping him or her from the life they would have had without me. For such a long time, I've been a secret that could not be shared. I've been tired for centuries, laddie. Now, I'll finally get my rest."

Gwyn remembered worrying about how hard Hermit was going to make his life in the future and his throat closed, burned by guilt. He pointed at the tablet-woven belt draped over the back of his desk chair. "Nothing else has changed. So, that was it? All I did was kill you?" He almost choked on the words.

"No, laddie. Do you think I'd trick you? Everything I've said is true. The curse was real and you've broken it. Releasing me from the counter-spell that kept me alive all these years is the proof."

"But Hermit, what's next? Won't the dragons come back?"

"The dragons come back? What gave you that idea? Magic has no power over death. Those who pass can never return." Hermit's voice grew stronger. "No Gwyn. The day of the dragons has long since passed. The curse was never that the dragons would disappear but that we'd be forgotten. And that's the only power we have over death, really, to keep those who are gone alive in our hearts."

"But what about the Holocene mass extinction? That's going to stop now, isn't it?"

Hermit shook his head. "Not by itself. Magic has no power over nature, either. In truth, nature doesn'a care. The earth will go on no matter who becomes extinct. It's happened before. Once, the skies were filled with dragons, pterosaurs as you call them. They lived for one hundred and sixty million years and then they were gone. Humans seem to think they'll survive forever, but the earth could easily go on without them."

Gwyn stared in disbelief. "Then what good did I do?"

"Gwyn, laddie, magic has power over one thing and one alone—mankind. It wasn'a nature that brought things to the state they are now, it was man. You've undone the curse that moved man away from nature, but what happens next willna depend on magic or nature—it will depend on man. It should be possible for mankind to forge new links with nature, but only if people do the work." Hermit closed his eyes. "I need a wee nap, if you dinna mind."

He fell into a sleep so deep that Gwyn was afraid to move. Hermit's breathing slowed until Gwyn felt sure it would stop. Downstairs, he heard his family getting ready for bed. He hoped Maddie might come up, but she didn't. Gwyn decided that was just as well. She'd be upset soon enough. The house fell silent.

Gwyn hated to get up, but finally, he had to use the bathroom. When he returned, Hermit moved close without waking, as if seeking comfort, so Gwyn stayed beside him, sometimes falling into an uneasy doze. He tried to brace himself for the worst, but when dawn broke, Hermit was still breathing.

CHAPTER TWENTY-THREE

THE WORLD INSIDE THE POND

Though Gwyn was afraid Hermit would not open his eyes again, he spoke before anyone else in the house had stirred. "I must get home," he said.

"You are home," Gwyn replied.

"No, not here, I must go back to Orkney. Can you take me to the water?"

Gwyn shook his head, trying to hold back his tears. "Hermit, you're not making sense. Orkney's across the ocean, thousands of kilometres away. You're too weak to fly."

The ghost of a twinkle crept into Hermit's eyes. "Never mind that, laddie. Can you take me to the water?"

Gwyn felt like someone had been hitting his head with a pillowcase filled with wet cement all night. His brain

269

would not work well enough to tell him what to do. I'm just a kid, he thought.

"Dad," he called. "Daddy, I need help." Even to his own ears, he sounded pathetic.

Gwyn watched both his parents draw back in horror when they saw Hermit, not just his father. The spell was truly broken. Maddie appeared just in time to see them react.

"Don't move, son. I'll get it off you," Tom said.

"No!" Maddie cried, rushing past to face him. "No, Dad, Gwyn's not in danger. This is Hermit, the Rae dragon."

"He's real?" Annette breathed the words. "You tried to tell me and I didn't believe you."

"He's real," Gwyn replied, "but I think he's dying."

"The Rae dragon?" Tom had gone pale. "How did you find him?"

"It's a long story. I'll tell you everything later, I promise, but now he needs our help. Please, Dad, will you help?" Gwyn was begging. He didn't care.

As Gwyn watched, his father came back to himself. "What can I do?"

"Take me to the water," Hermit croaked. "To the pond where I flew, just take me there, please?"

o o o

St. John's is a city of long Saturday nights and late Sunday mornings. The streets were empty. As they drove toward the lake, Gwyn saw one bleary-eyed guy in a leather jacket who looked as if he was just coming home from his night out. Nobody walked around the lake at seven in the morning. As they drove into the parking lot at Quidi Vidi, Gwyn noticed that the clouds out at sea had gathered to make a kind of false dawn over the eastern horizon, turning the sky pink. The air was windless, as if the world were holding its breath, and all around them ice was melting.

Gwyn and Maddie lifted Hermit from the car while Annette rushed ahead. "Oh my," she called. "I've never seen anything like this. Come and look."

Yesterday's mild weather had melted the top of the ice on Quidi Vidi, leaving a smooth silver layer beneath. With no wind to ruffle it, the whole lake was now a perfect mirror. Each seagull on the water stood on an upside-down twin; even the ones in the air were matched by flying images. The shore was edged above and below the waterline with perfect trees, one ring pointing up, one pointing down. It was like standing at the edge of a bottomless canyon, and Gwyn swayed when he saw it.

"Steady, son," Tom said, never taking his eyes off Hermit.

Maybe it was the car ride or maybe the company, but Hermit had revived a little. "I'm pleased to finally make your acquaintance, Thomas," he said. "You've a great deal of Daniel about you."

Gwyn's father nodded, speechless.

"Why did you want to come here?" Gwyn asked.

"Last night, as I slept, I dreamed of this place. It seemed to call to me. I'm no sorry to be going to my rest, laddie. Try to understand."

A sudden breeze rippled through the air, then it was gone.

"Look! Something's happened to the lake," Annette said as the water stilled and Hermit launched himself into the air. Gwyn cried out, certain Hermit wouldn't have the strength to fly, but the small dragon climbed steadily. He hovered for a moment, proud against the sky, then dove for the lake.

"Hermit! No!" Maddie screamed, but he folded his wings like a falcon. His reflection did the same as it rose from the water to meet him. He's going to hit the ice, Gwyn thought, and he braced for a sickening thud, but it never came. Instead, when Hermit touched his reflection, the light seemed to shudder, and where there had been two Hermits, the dragon and his reflection, there was only one, an upside-down dragon, making for a shore that did not belong to Quidi Vidi. That sky was summer blue, the trees gone. Gwyn could see gently sloping grassy fields and, in the distance, purple hills. Near the shore where

Hermit was heading were strange bumps made of stone and thatch with smoke rising from them, and Gwyn realized they might be houses.

Another puff of wind wrinkled the surface of the water. When the reflection reappeared, it looked just as it should. The mirror was still extraordinary in its perfection, but it was a natural wonder.

Maddie sobbed in her mother's arms, but Gwyn felt as if his tears had already been cried. He turned to his father. "We have a lot to tell you."

o o o

The Rae family spent the rest of the day in the kitchen, mostly talking, sometimes eating. Maddie and Gwyn took turns as the whole story came out, bit by bit. Annette frowned when Gwyn told them how he'd stolen the twelve weaving tablets and given them back to Sunny. "You're lucky we know Sunny so well," she said. Gwyn wasn't sure it was luck. Things had come together so neatly. He didn't say this, though.

When Gwyn tried to explain why he'd had to make the weaving, Tom shook his head. "I can't accept this idea, of curses and counter-spells. Somehow this little pterosaur survived but there must be a natural explanation. If only I'd had a chance to study him."

Maddie and Gwyn exchanged a look, and Gwyn wondered if it was just accidental that Hermit had missed the generations between Daniel and them.

"But where did he go?" Maddie asked when they'd finally finished the story.

"He said he wanted to go home to Orkney," Gwyn replied.

"Then maybe that's where he went," Annette said. "Those distant hills were such a pretty colour, I thought they were covered in heather."

"I saw houses," Gwyn added, "by the shore, made of stone and grass, but they didn't look like any houses I'd ever seen. Did you see them?" No one else had.

It was only six in the evening, but Gwyn could not stop yawning.

"I'll make some supper, and you'd better call it a day," his mother said. "You lost a lot of sleep last night."

With his family Gwyn had felt almost normal, but his bedroom was an empty socket. This was where Hermit ought to be, asking crazy questions about science, demanding a tidier room. It seemed to Gwyn as if a black hole had opened in the middle of his life and nothing would ever be the same. He fell into bed but found he could not sleep. After tossing and turning for a few hours, he heard someone creeping up the stairs and turned to find Maddie.

"You're still awake?" she asked.

Gwyn nodded. "I'm beat but my mind won't stop."

She almost sat on Gwyn's desk chair, but the tablet-woven belt stopped her. "This is what you wove?"

Gwyn nodded again. He'd shown it to no one. It seemed too private and strange.

"It's beautiful," Maddie said, running her fingers over the weave. She held it while she sat down, carefully, as if it were a living thing. "I've been thinking about what happened this morning. Hermit went back to Orkney, but he didn't just show up over there today. Did he?"

"I don't think so. It seemed to be summer, and those houses looked like something from a long time ago."

She nodded. "Remember what Hermit told us about all the other dragons and how they'd disappeared?" Her eyes grew bright with excitement. "Maybe he went wherever they did. Do you think that's possible?"

Gwyn considered for a moment. "I hope so. I hate to think of him dying alone. Maybe there was someone in those houses who would take care of him."

"I hope so too. We'll never forget him."

Maddie put the tablet-woven band down on Gwyn's desk, gave a shaky sigh and left. She was right, of course. They would never forget him. And he'd want it that way. What was it he'd said? The only power we have over death is to keep the ones who are gone alive in our hearts.

They'd do that for him. But what about the dragons? Would anyone else ever know they were not the evil, mythical beings the Vikings had hated? It was hard to see how that would ever change.

Gwyn waited for sleep, hoping Hermit might come to him in a dream, but when he finally drifted off, his sleep was dreamless.

o o o

Night after night, Gwyn hoped Hermit might appear in his dreams, but that didn't happen. The cold, wet spring dragged on as April passed, and gradually Gwyn learned to enjoy life again. He walked around the lake with his field glasses and, if he ran into Tyler Cull, they smiled as they passed. Once the ice was gone, Gwyn hiked the path that hugged the Narrows below Signal Hill, where cormorants dove for fish and dried their ragged wings in the sun and, farther out, nesting ravens flew like aerial acrobats. The humpback whales returned, and one day, Gwyn sat on the top of a cliff on Signal Hill watching them swim below, the seawater turning their white pectoral fins aqua blue.

When Gwyn's father finished teaching, he said, "I'm going to fast-track my summer research. By the time you get out of school, I'll be able to spend a few hours with you each day."

Gwyn smiled. He'd already started looking around to find out about the mass extinction on his own, but he knew his father would make everything go ten times faster. Still, nothing had changed. Maybe Hermit was wrong. He went over their conversations again and again, wondering what it would be like to watch everyone else grow old and die. He couldn't shake the thought so, one day in June, he went to the drugstore and bought a box of chocolates. A few days later, after school, he went to the Mews Annex.

"Oh, it's you," Dr. Mews said when he answered Gwyn's knock. "Come in."

The Mews Annex was a mess, with half-filled boxes everywhere. "What's going on?" Gwyn asked.

"Everything's moving into The Rooms," Dr. Mews replied. "I decided it was counterproductive to split the collection up like this."

Gwyn smiled. Daniel's papers were going to be housed in the same building as the weaving tablets. He wished he could tell Hermit. Then he took a closer look at Dr. Mews, who seemed even smaller than Gwyn remembered, somehow deflated. "Are you going to work there?"

The old man shook his head. "No, I'm too old to make such a big change. I've decided to retire."

That sounded like an even bigger change to Gwyn, but he didn't say so. Instead, he held out the chocolates.

"I'm glad I caught you, then. I wanted to apologize for being so rude about dragons."

Dr. Mews took the chocolates. "Well, thank you. It didn't stop me from voting for your project, you know."

"It didn't?"

"Of course not! It was a fine piece of research. One of the other judges didn't appreciate how many hours you'd spent with the archival materials. I'm not allowed to talk about it, of course," he paused for a moment, then added, "but Dr. O'Donnell understood."

Gwyn laughed. "It's okay. The guy who won is in my class. Winning mattered a lot more to him. Anyway, I learned other things."

"How to control your temper?"

"Maybe not that." Gwyn smiled as he shook his head.

"Funny," Dr. Mews said, "I was thinking about you the other day while I was reading a website I follow, Archival World News."

"A website?"

"Yes, a website. A person has to move with the times. It seems they just found a fabulous manuscript about dragons some place in Scotland where they've been excavating for a few years. Tarbot? Tarbat? Yes, I think it's called Tarbat, the site of a monastery. They think it was Pictish, which is highly unusual, the only one they've ever found, and they've unearthed an ancient illuminated manuscript full of stories about dragons. The survival of this manuscript was described as miraculous. It was found in a sealed wooden box inside a stone chamber. The trench they were digging almost missed it. It's written in Latin, and they said it was very odd because the dragons weren't enemies in the stories, they were heroes. They're calling it an epic advance in their understanding of Pictish folklore."

"Folklore!" The word flew out before Gwyn could stop himself.

Dr. Mews smiled. "Of course. What else could it be?" He opened the box of chocolates. "Would you like one?"

Gwyn took a deep breath. There was no point in trying to tell Dr. Mews this wasn't just folklore. They'd only fight again. He took a chocolate and Dr. Mews put the box down.

"Aren't you going to have one?" Gwyn asked.

"I'm diabetic, but I appreciate the thought."

Gwyn sat down. "So, what are you going to do when you retire?"

Dr. Mews was happy to talk about his plans to travel to Greece, Egypt and Turkey. He'd done a lot of research.

When Gwyn left the Mews Annex, he congratulated himself. A few months ago, the idea that the manuscript had been found and misunderstood would have made him go ballistic. Now, he could accept it as the first piece in a puzzle that might take decades to assemble.

That night, finally, Gwyn dreamed about Hermit. He was flying with other dragons, over a lake that nestled among treeless green hills, free, as he was always meant to be. The dragons played tag, then flew in slow, deliberate patterns that looked like dances. Gwyn could feel the stiff breeze and, though it was out of sight, he smelled the sea. This place looked like dragon heaven. Suddenly, though Gwyn had heard nothing, all the dragons turned and flew to the ground as if they had been called, landing at the feet of someone who looked eerily familiar, with Gwyn's own skinny frame and pale blond curls. Even before their eyes met and the boy gave him a grave, joyful nod, Gwyn knew he was not dreaming about himself. He woke smiling.

That was another sign, but it wasn't easy to be patient. Every day, Gwyn searched his father's online science journals for more proof that the Viking curse had been undone. He found nothing, not a clue, as the Holocene mass extinction began to come into focus for him. It was every bit as big and scary as it had seemed that day when Gwyn and Hermit first discovered it, and, outside the scientific community, nobody seemed to know it was happening. Gwyn began to realize he'd need friends, lots and lots of them, if he was ever going to change things. He had no idea where they would come from. He just allowed himself to believe they'd appear in time.

Soon, a wall in Tom's study was covered in pictures

of mammals, insects, amphibians and reptiles joined to places on a map of the world by lines of wool Gwyn and his father had borrowed from Maddie, along with charts and graphs depicting population declines. They worked so hard, Annette began to complain.

"Enough," she announced one Saturday, walking into Tom's study, where they both sat hunched over their computers. "You can't spend the whole summer inside. I'm taking a week off and we're going to visit the Viking site at L'Anse aux Meadows. Jonas is coming too. I've already cleared it with his parents."

"Maddie's leaving Hollywood?" Gwyn asked.

His mother smiled. "Maddie's told them she's unavailable for a week."

"Hollywood" was what Maddie called the independent film productions she and her new friends helped to crew, dragging lights and cables around and standing by traffic barricades so the filmmakers could work in the streets. It sounded dead boring to Gwyn, but she couldn't stop talking about it.

Though Gwyn had always loved that trip, this summer it seemed like a waste of time. He could hardly bear to stop working.

A few days later, taking a break from packing, Gwyn found a small item in *New Scientist* under the heading "Archaeology."

"Strange bone unearthed on Mainland Island, Orkney." Gwyn's eyes raced ahead. ". . . a long, thin bone, the kind normally only associated with pterosaurs, though not fossilized. Tests are being conducted to see if the bone's origin can be determined." Gwyn smiled. "Not fossilized" meant the bone was recent. He wondered how long it would take for them to put two and two together, to connect the Tarbat manuscript with the bones. Plural, he thought, because he was sure they were going to find more.

Gwyn's room was a mess, and he smiled to think what Hermit would say if he could see it. He scooped an almost clean T-shirt off the floor. As he threw it into his pack, the weaving he'd made with the ancient tablets caught his eye, pinned to the wall above his desk. Gwyn shook his head, remembering how he'd expected it to fix everything right away. He was just beginning to understand what that weaving really meant. When he'd unwoven the curse from the past, he'd woven himself into a promise, for the planet, for the future. If he was going to spend the rest of his life fighting to accomplish the impossible, maybe he deserved a few days off. As for the impossible, it could happen — he already knew that.

ACKNOWLEDGEMENTS

The author would like to thank the Newfoundland and Labrador Arts Council for generous funding through its Professional Project Grants Program.